A SE
OF LOSS

A SENSE
OF LOSS

& OTHER STORIES

Martin Foreman

GMP

First published February 1993 by GMP Publishers Ltd
P O Box 247, London N17 9QR, England

World Copyright © 1993 Martin Foreman

A CIP catalogue record for this book
is available from the British Library

ISBN 0 85449 185 6

Distributed in North America by InBook
P O Box 120470, East Haven, CT 06512, USA

Distributed in Australia by Bulldog Books
P O Box 155, Broadway, NSW 2007, Australia

Printed and bound in the EC on environmentally-friendly paper
by Nørhaven A/S, Viborg, Denmark

For Erik, a promise kept

CONTENTS

Room With No View	9
The Dowager and I	21
The Coming of Santa Claus	29
It was, I suppose, inevitable	35
Ganymede	45
Triangle	61
A Room to Let	73
Discotheque — Four Voices	83
Train of Events	97
Simon's Dinner Party	103
The Benefactor	113
Oblivion	135
An Odd Fellow	153
For the first time in your life, Andrew	161
A Sense of Loss	169

ROOM WITH NO VIEW

I hate this room. I hate the fact that it is always dark, that on days when the sun actually lies for an hour or so at the foot of the bed I must close the curtain against the curiosity of passers-by. I hate the dirt that lies thick where it cannot be seen, the grease stains that I cannot remove, the peeling and grubby paint. I hate this room because it is my room, because it is all I have, because no matter how far into the future I look I can see nothing but these four walls, this ceiling, that door. I hate this room because it is nothing, has nothing, not even a prospect, not even a view.

He lies here asleep, breathing so lightly that the cover does not move. His head and shoulders and an arm sprawl across the pillow, showing me the spots that lie thick on his back. When I first saw him I looked with more curiosity than desire, impressed only by the thick black hair that swept up and back and tapered like an arrow. He caught my stare and for some reason grinned; without thinking, a reflex from the past, from countless nights in bars and discos, I winked and saw him wink back.

When we came in, I wanted to rush into the bathroom, to shower away two days of dirt and endless weeks of loneliness, but he held me and kissed me and sniffed me as urgently as if he were seeking something of great value, something he believed that I somewhere had. I tried to respond, but I had forgotten how love could be made and could only watch his pale, elongated body as it emerged from its clothes, his hands as they undid and pulled off my trousers and shirt, his expression as he pushed and pummelled me this way and that, as he moved frantically over me, as his mouth hung open in a deepening silent cry, as his hips and body jerked, electrocuted by some unseen torturer. I stared, amazed, for I could not remember anyone coming like that, anyone so racked, anyone so lost. I envied him, I envied whatever took him out of himself, out of his world, out of this room.

Now the pall of sex lies thick and warm. If I could somehow touch it, hold it, concentrate it, inhale it, I would understand what moved him, what possessed him, this strange secret he has. Did I ever make love like that? Did I ever lose myself, surrender myself so completely? I cannot remember. I cannot even remember those I have made love to; I see only disconnected faces, bodies, buttocks and groins.

He sits opposite me at the other end of the bed drinking tea. We have made love again, slowly, intensely, our bodies coming together like a strong tide, each individual movement a scarcely noticed ripple of waves. This time I was swept up, I had to take part. He hypnotised me with the staring eye that came together in the middle of his face as we kissed, his tongue pressing deeper and deeper into my mouth, pushing me back onto the bed and forcing me to close my eyes and give myself to him. And as the orgasm, the tide, came near, I did not know whether it came from within me or without and I felt myself explode and I wanted to cry and when it was over I had to hold him and hold him and hold him until the swirling had died, my body had become whole again and I was no longer afraid to open my eyes.

His name is Eric, he once worked in a bakery, he usually signs on the day before I do. He lives not far from here, with his parents, no longer tries to look for work, spends his days listening to music, wandering the streets, combing his hair. His voice is quiet and heavy with accent, suggests strength and anger and pride. He frowns, doesn't like being questioned, asks no questions in return. Curiosity, I realise, is no more than a habit, an impulse which destroys as much as it explains. The more I ask him about the outside world, the more I remind him of it and encourage him to return. So I stop, say nothing, watch and wait.

He tells me he is hungry and asks if I have food. The cupboard is beside him; there is, as always, pasta and baked beans. I can find an old tomato and cheese. He stands watching as I cook and without turning my eye I see the arch of his nose, the roughness of his chin and cheek, the thin and hard body that waits, that calls out to me from under his shirt, his prick, long, curved and almost deformed, the hair that curls, as if surprised by itself, all over his buttocks and legs. But that is only part of him; it bothers me that I cannot remember whether his body was warm or cold, that I have forgotten his smell, which now lies buried under the steam of macaroni and sauce.

He squats on the bed, plate in hand, as I fiddle with the aerial; I join him and we watch the cartoon and I am surprised to realise that the day has gone, it is late afternoon. He watches intently, laughing at the absurdities on the screen, only occasionally looking down to guide food onto his fork. Because he laughs, I laugh with him and these talking cats, these black and grey figures, are not only comic but erotic, pervaded with his presence, his body, his lust. I reach out a hand and place it on his knee. He ignores it. I move it down, into his thigh, and squeeze. He makes no response but I sense his tension and quickening of breath.

We have watched everything, game shows and comedies, soap operas and the news. We have moved our bodies again and again, searching for the ideal position of comfort with each other and the bed. Now he is stretched out on his front, head propped up by the pillow and his hands. I kneel over him, staring at each fold of his shirt, at the stains and tears in his trousers. His body focuses at the curve of his rump, drawing my eyes and hands. I touch it, hold it, stroke it. He raises his hips to let me reach in under his stomach, release the button and zip and pull his trousers down to his thighs. I push up the shirt and reveal the buttocks; the suggestion of muscle, the abstract pattern of hair, the shadow that glides down to bury itself between his legs, is all so beautiful, so breath-taking, that I am almost afraid to go on.

He is in the bathroom, preparing for the night. I don't want anyone to see him, to frown or smile, to remind him that there are others but me. As I was making love and he lay hardly responding I thought I heard him cry. Do you want me to stop, I asked. "No," he said, "no, no," almost desperately, like a plea. When I came, collapsed and rolled off him, he pulled my face to his and kissed me and kissed me with a harsher urgency than when we first came in. "I love you," he whispered and I wondered if I had heard.

We lie squashed together in the dark and he asks the kind of questions that I asked him before, I tell him about my family, that I don't see them anymore. "Why?" Because they live two hundred miles away, because we've never been close, because they're part of a past which is long dead and gone. I tell him about university and the fact that I've only ever had summer jobs. "What kind of work d'you want?" The question is strange; I don't know. Months, years ago, I used to write to companies, to libraries, to newspapers, to advertising agencies, but they all turned me down. I no longer think about work, hardly know what it means.

He asks about those I've slept with before. In the days when I had money I would go out every night to pick someone up, but I've never lived with anyone, never seen the same person more than a few times. He finds that strange, tells me about the girl he went out with for over a year and the boy who lived in the same block, who played football every week. Then he stops, unwilling to talk any more, puts an arm round my chest, rests his head between my shoulder and the pillow and soon, very soon, is asleep.

I do not know how long I have been staring up at the ceiling. There is little to see but thick shadow; all the stains and marks I look at in daytime have gone. I am not comfortable — he has pushed me into the corner, yet still grasps my waist — but that is not the reason why I cannot sleep. The room has changed; its walls and curtains are the same, its heavy furniture still presses into the middle, the carpet, so old that its pattern has faded, is no less ugly. I used to feel oppressed, weighed down, but that feeling has gone. I feel somehow lighter, a little less real.

I can just make him out in the darkness, his hair crushed and tangled on the pillow, a suggestion of beard on his cheek, his mouth half-open as he breathes the undertone of sleep. Now I notice his smell, strong, like an animal, swaying between arousal and repulsion. His body stretches forever beneath the covers and each position he shifts into is more attractive, more sexual than the last.

My emotions are frozen. I dare not think or remind myself I am alone. He promised to come back. I don't know if he will. Only to go home, to change his clothes, he said, both pleading and defiance in his voice. I watched him through the window, saw him somehow transfigured as he walked away. I felt I had died when I could no longer see him. Perhaps I never will again.

I should tidy up, put some order in the room, make it attractive. I look around me and wonder where to begin. Bed, wardrobe, cooker, chair all stare back at me defiantly, challenging me to move them, clean them, create a better home. There is no point. With one of my last coins I go and shower, wash away the dirt, the smell and the past.

I did not realise how handsome he could be. His face has resolved into angles of personality, he has shaved and redone his hair and put on bright clothes. "Take this," he says, handing me a carrier bag, then puts his arms around me and we kiss. My tongue probes, my hands begin to feel under his belt, but he draws away and asks, "Well, aren't you going to have a look?" I open and pull out packets and cans and vegetables and at first I do not understand, then he tells me that he borrowed money from his sister, that it is a present, that it means we do not have to go out. An image of the street, of shops and queues, of people talking and moving and jostling, of trying to understand money and how much I have and how much I can spend, returns like the memory of an unpleasant dream.

We have soup and sausages and potatoes and eggs. As we eat, I look up from the bed to see someone peering in. A woman's face, turning away as she walks by, its foreignness frightening and threatening. I stand up, look out at the brick wall, the rusty railings, the dull grey sky; it has always been a prison sentence, never a view. I close the curtain in anger and resentment, switch on the light and TV. The news is on; there are demonstrations, a bomb has exploded somewhere. I do not quite understand, as if it is all in a language I once knew but have forgotten.

I suggest coffee, but he does not want it. Instead, he comes over and stands before me, stares as he takes off his jacket and shirt, lets his trousers and pants fall to the floor, holds me with his eyes as he kicks them away. I do not know what to do, I do not know what he wants. I look down and up from his groin to his stare, his expression so deep and painful that I am afraid to speak, to ask what is wrong. Then, as if suddenly released, I drop to my knees, grasp his buttocks and pull his prick, his body, into my mouth as deep as I can.

He has fallen onto the bed, his eyes are closed, he trembles and breathes as if he were dying and I was the one who had killed him. I watch for a moment, then open my jeans, straddle his chest and force myself into him. He chokes, but does not push me away.

The television voices go on and on. As I open my eyes I realise I have been asleep. In alarm I sit up, but he is there, in the chair. He looks at me, I think he smiles. I lie down again, sink back into the warmth, protected by his presence, the duvet, the room.

He makes tea, turns down the television, comes to sit on the bed. "Sleep well?" But he is not interested in the answer; there is a weight within him, the weight of something he has to say.

"Do you like doing it with me?" he eventually asks. The question surprises me; I tell him yes. He says nothing. I wait. "I can't do it often enough," he half-grins in apology. "You're the first person who hasn't complained, who wants to do it with me all the time. The others . . . they wanted to talk or fall in love or tell me what to do. You just want to do it." He looks thoughtful, serious.

"I don't want to stop. I want to do it again *now*." He doesn't move, but I feel my own reaction, look down at the black trousers that cover his. "I want to do everything." Everything? "Everything," he insists, "whatever there is to do. Do you know what I mean?" I nod, and an impression, vague and formless, enters my mind, shimmering with fear and anticipation.

But does he understand? Carefully, gently, afraid of asking the question or making the statement that might scare him away, from me, from this room, I talk about what is possible, what others have done. He listens carefully and I watch his expression as a yachtsman his compass — too much in the wrong direction and he frowns, when I am on the right track his eyes open wider. Thus I learn he would not welcome ropes or chains, blows or pain, insults or humiliation. Nor does he want to dress up, to parade in uniform or costume. It is the body itself that enthralls him, its reactions and limits, how far one can penetrate, what makes the penis swell, what causes each sensation. You can go on and on, I tell him, even die. "How?" he asks, and I tell him of strangulation, its diversion of blood to the groin from the brain, of mass murderers, of the pornography of death and his eyes are bright and I watch and talk to him with no feelings at all.

He waits until I have finished, then throws himself on me, his lips crashing into mine, his hands kneading my back, burrowing under my shirt, his sex, muffled by his clothes, battering into mine. For a moment it is like the first time, I can only yield, not react, then I feel a rush so violent that it is almost anger and I push him off, roll onto him and we fight for dominance as our mouths scrape each other's necks and our hands and knees and feet kick off each other's clothes. I win, because I am heavier and for a moment I lie across him, see his flushed and eager face, his thin body with its few muscles and scattering of dark hairs and I want less to make love with him than to become him and I fall and try to enter him with not just my mouth and prick, but with all my flesh, all my weight.

We fought and attacked and resisted like samurai, Greek wrestlers, heroes in war. We lie here panting, two duelling stags exhausted but not defeated, the noise of our breathing filling the room. I entered him again, tried to pierce with my seed not just his body but his heart, yet despite all my efforts, my fury and lust, we are as apart from each other as we were before. I will not accept this separation which defies my will; I grab him and pull him to me and kiss him with the same fierceness as before. He responds as urgently and we move over and against and with each other with undiminished energy but greater cunning, knowing that the lust, the aggression and desire, has been freed from our groins and now lurks in every cell of our bodies. This love-making mocks, intimidates and challenges; with no orgasm to offer, it taunts us to search out other, hidden sensations.

It is the middle of the night. The radio plays quietly, there is only an American film on television. He sits up in bed, wearing an old sweater of mine, as I prepare another meal. He is in the mood to talk again, asks about the others who live in the house. I hardly know them, I say shortly, some I have never seen. Others have families and friends and jobs, yet stay here for years; when I pass them in the corridor I no longer make the effort to smile. "And the landlord?" I hardly remember him; he is only the name on the cheque.

I want to know about the boy who played football, what kind of person he was, what his body was like. His description is vague, tells me little more than they "did it" once or twice a week. "He was a bit funny, though. He never wanted to come. He used to get mad if it lasted less than an hour." What happened? Why did you stop? "He got nicked." It takes me a moment to recognise the expression. And the girl? He shrugs and tells me even less.

We lie and listen to the music and the disc jockey's quiet voice. Our hands wander over each other as uninhibited as children in their favourite playground. It becomes a rhythm, music, each limb, each muscle a different instrument, each stroke a separate note. The arms are woodwind, the chest a drum, fingers are piccolo and flute. I will play all night; I do not want to sleep. I never want to sleep again.

Coming back from the bathroom he hands me an envelope. "Is this you?" It is the giro. "We're going to need it," he says.

I look down and see that his face is red and there are tears in his eyes. He makes frantic signs that tell me not to stop. I grasp his head again and push and push. What I feel is not my rapid breath but his choking, not my melting but his struggling for air. I remember taking him in my mouth, always wanting more than he can give. I push harder, harder, and his grunts are the sound of my orgasm.

The picture wobbles and there is a faint smell of burning from the back of the set. Annoyed, I switch it off.

When he moves inside me, I am the footballer who does not want him to come, who does not want him to stop. I lie in his shadow as if under the angel of death; he stares at me like a scientist watching a drugged animal. It becomes a contest to see who can make the other come. I resist and resent the explosion that threatens to destroy me, try to hold it back with clenched fists and face tight with anger, but there is nothing I can do; I will lose again.

We have no food. I refuse to go out. I sign the giro and give it to him, together with a list of the shopping we need. After he leaves, I believe even less that he will come back.

A noise startles me. I raise my head from the bed and see him turn on the television, put packets and cans away. When he has finished, he wants to go and have a shower. I tell him no, lift him and place him on the bed, lick him all over, lick him clean, lick him dry.

He arches his back, splays out his limbs, demands that I push his legs still further apart. His muscles strain, reflected in his grimace. We are both dissatisfied; to me it is a display of gymnastics, nothing more, to him a failed experiment.

He wants an erection that will last for ever. I take a shoelace and pull it tight until the flesh goes purple and I fear the protruding veins will burst. "Now, make me come," he orders, "make me come!" he repeats when I hesitate. I take hold of him, but it is like rubbing leather. I close my eyes and when I hear him groan and feel the liquid spatering into my mouth, I am afraid to taste and discover it is blood. It is only sperm; I am relieved but he is disappointed, for his sex is already shrinking and loosening its bond.

He would do anything for me, to me, that I asked. But it would mean little to either of us, for it is his body I want, his own sensations he needs. So on we go, he leading, I following, scarcely aware of each step we take.

The television has finally broken down. I miss its light, its endless images.

He wants more, he always wants more than I can give. "Your hand," he pleaded, "your hand." At last I yielded and, trembling more than he, let him guide it in. He cried, silently, tears overflowing, and looked at me with what I could only under-stand was pain and longing. Now he lies exhausted and I stare at his body and stare at my hand, thinking of what I have done, of what I could have done, and my emotions are blank.

In the half-light I stare at the curtain and remember the world outside, the pavement and the street, the people and buses and cars which go by. Dogs sniff there, litter is blown, children cry; traffic growls, shops yawn, buildings glare at each other and threaten to topple. The window should not exist, should be solid wall; the glass and the curtain make us too vulnerable, too open to the winds and the wrath of the world. Even the corridor worries me, the stairs up and the passage that takes us to the bathroom. Behind each door is a hostile face, an accusing voice.

I am losing weight. My body is becoming thinner and more attractive. He plays with it, licking and kneading and massaging as he did on the first day.

"If I died, would you die with me?" he asks. I look at him uncertainly, not sure what to say.

I have dreamt of my parents. They were dressed in Edwardian costume and my mother offered me tea. My father asked about my studies and gave me advice. I did not understand and he repeated his words. As they drifted away I loved them more and more.

He lies across the bed. I kneel at his head and we kiss, my eyes open, taking in the strange angle of his body. He stops and whispers he loves me. This time I know I have heard. I have nothing to say. I hope he never tells me again.

I come back from the shower and realise that the room stinks, the furniture is grimy and the sheets are dirty with semen and sweat. He sprawls on the chair, reading a book. It seems as if he has always been there; I cannot remember how I lived before he came, how I would live if he went. He is part of my body, the meaning of my life, my soul, my albatross. I look down at his body, the mess of his hair, his pale and spotted skin, the jumble of flesh at his groin, the awkward knees and feet. I wonder what his attraction was, what it still is. I want to be alone again, but I do not want him to leave. I cannot live without him and will no longer live with him. I will no longer live.

   I lean over, he drops the book and reaches for me, rubbing gently and delicately until I am hard. Then his other hand guides me to his thighs, looks up as I let it rest there.

   We make love more slowly than ever before. In the middle he

asks if there is anything wrong. I start to say no, then tell him I think it'll soon be the last time. He seems to understand; I hope he does.

THE
DOWAGER
AND I

It was Philip who introduced me to the Dowager, shortly after my arrival in London. "A wonderful woman," he enthused, negotiating with difficulty Hammersmith's one-way system. "She's over sixty now and doesn't get about so much, but she used to be the toast of London."

"Why do you call her the Dowager?" I asked, youthful pride preventing me from enquiring exactly what the title meant.

"Everyone does. Of course she isn't a real Dowager, but she's one of nature's aristocrats. No money, poor woman. It's quite sad. You'd think the state would pay her to give an audience twice a week. A sort of Citizen's Advice Bureau for people like you and me. A highly specialised agony aunt." He laughed at the idea and I smiled with him.

"Sigurd will be there," Philip went on. "He's the artist I told you about, from Norway. Desperately unlucky. He never sells anything. When he does, he spends it all on drink. But he's devoted to the Dowager and doing her portrait for her, free."

To a young man for whom reality a month before had stretched no further than the streets and bars of various Yorkshire towns, this verbal picture of genteel poverty and frustrated artistic genius appealed as much as any photograph of deserted tropical beaches or yachts crowding some Mediterranean harbour. The steep cracked steps down to the basement of a converted Victorian house and the flaking paint and dirt enhanced the romantic image, as did the tall dishevelled figure who opened the door.

"This is Sigurd," Philip introduced, but I was barely acknowledged before the Norwegian disappeared back down the corridor muttering that he was always being interrupted in the middle of work.

I followed Philip into the living-room, where the old lady sat upright in a high, narrow chair, her dingy surroundings set off by her light blue dress. It looked expensive to my inexperienced eye, while the large cameo at her neck impressed with its size. The make-up was obvious, yet not out of place.

"My dear Dowager," said Philip, striding forward, grasping the hands and kissing the proffered cheek. "You look marvellous."

"So do you, Philip, dear." The voice creaked, underlain with an accent I later recognised as Hackney. "And who is this?" she turned to me with a knowing smile.

"Paul, meet the Dowager."

I stretched out my hand. "How do you do?"

"How do you do? Such a polite young man," she addressed Philip. "So upright and handsome."

"Isn't he?" I began to blush. "The portrait, Sigurd. Let us see it!"

"No, no." Sigurd moved as if to defend the easel over which he had draped a cloth. "No one sees it before it is ready." He was a gangling individual whose beard, without moustache, did little to hide his weak face.

"Sigurd did these." The Dowager — the word was still strange to me — gestured at the paintings on the wall. Each showed a few ragged flowers stuck awkwardly into a two-dimensional vase. They reminded me of the pictures my sister had drawn as a child.

"Now sit down beside me, Paul," the Dowager insisted, patting the arm of the sofa. "I want to talk to you. You're staying with Philip, aren't you?"

"For the moment. Until I find a place of my own."

"Oh, I hope that won't happen." Her smile was both gracious and confiding. "After all, why move if you're happy there?"

I wasn't sure what to reply.

"You know, I've been wanting to meet you for weeks, to see if everything Philip has said to me is true. And I think it is."

"What has he said?" I asked, both annoyed and curious. I glanced over to the window where he stood listening to a diatribe from Sigurd.

"Only nice things, I can assure you. And they must be true." Her voice lowered and she beckoned me to listen closer. "Because he's changed so much. I used to be terribly worried about him, you know. He was desperately unhappy."

I was puzzled. "But he's always very cheerful with me. I've never seen him depressed."

"That's because you've changed him. I know about these things." She sat upright again, regaining her imperial expression. "I know so many young men like you and Philip." I refrained from commenting that Philip was hardly young. "I've been very lucky. Some of them have been very good to me. I've been able to help them too. You can when you're old and can see things like I do. You will be a friend of mine, won't you?"

"Yes," I said, intrigued and uncertain, for I had never met anyone like her before.

"I'm so glad. How old are you?"

"Twenty."

"That *is* very young. Oh, it's a marvellous age, but so confused. You'll let me help you when I can, won't you? Give you advice? You don't have to take it, you know."

Although I felt patronised, as all young people do when it is suggested they are not in control of their lives, I told her yes, of course I would.

"What are you two talking about?" Philip came over. "Dowager, have you been corrupting this innocent here?"

"Not at all, Philip. You know I wouldn't corrupt anyone."

"As long as you know he's mine." There was an arm round my shoulder and I thought I could smell bad breath.

"The Dowager was very taken with you," Philip informed me on the way home. "She wants to meet you again soon."

"I liked her," I said. Indeed, I had been fascinated by the old lady so at home in the midst of such an odd trio.

Within the week there was a phone call inviting me to tea. "How lovely to see you," she said at the door. "Goodness, I had forgotten how tall you were. Come in." She was wearing dull red, with a string of pearls and heavy pendants at her ears. I noticed she moved unsteadily, with one hand against the wall or a table for support.

"How do you like it?" she asked in the living-room, pointing to the painting hanging above the mantelpiece. The grey hair and pink face were more diagrammatic than representational; any old woman, even a man, could have been portrayed.

"It's nice," I said, trying to smile.

"Isn't it beautiful? I feel quite honoured. As you can see, I've given it pride of place." There was no irony in her voice; I did not know whether to pity her poor taste or applaud her loyalty.

"How is Philip?" she asked once we were seated and with cups in our hands.

"He's fine."

"I'm so glad to hear it. And you? Are you happy?"

"Of course." It was not so great a lie; I was not unhappy.

"You must learn to understand Philip, you know. He's a good man, a good man indeed. You mustn't mind his moods. It's his privilege as an artist." Philip was a teacher who had had one or two poems printed; he had also written a novel which no one would publish.

"Have you got a job yet?"

"Yes. I start next week."

"Oh, good, what kind of job?"

"In an advertising agency. I'm not sure what I'll be doing."

"Will it lead to greater things?"

"I hope so."

"I'll keep my fingers crossed."

As a child I would have been irritated by her tone, but now I pitied her efforts to please. For me, age was like paralysis or blindness, a tragedy which struck only a few. The relief that I was not a victim let me be generous, let me forgive her trespasses on my dignity.

"You know, you remind me of someone I knew years ago, probably before you were born. He looked like you, but was much . . ." she searched for the word, "rougher. He worked in the docks or somewhere like that. I was quite shy of him at first, but he had a heart of gold. He went to live with another friend of mine."

"And?" I prompted when the story seemed to have stopped.

"That's all. But what I mean is, I hope *you* have a heart of gold. You're so quiet, it's difficult to tell. Don't hurt Philip, will you?"

What about him hurting me? I wondered. "I'll try not to."

"Good," she smiled. "I'm giving you the benefit of my experience, don't you see? To help you. There was another boy I knew, called David. I could tell from the start he was a bad sort. Charming manners, but he didn't fool me."

So the conversation went on. She darted to and fro between the topic of Philip and myself and other people she knew, frowning or laughing as she recalled some incident that she only half-explained. Her questions were intimate — how much was Philip drinking, how did we spend each evening — and the need to stop and think gave insights into our relationship like windows being opened in a long-closed room. Furthermore, I was fascinated by the glimpses into other lives. There were couples who first met in the unlikeliest places and stayed loyal through the worst of crises. Simple bus rides became races against time, while a thoughtless telephone call threatened to ruin a life forever. Separations, whether mutual or embittered, were always accompanied by tears. I listened, rapt, while the Dowager's eyes sparkled with one man's happiness and narrowed at another's treachery.

Over the next few months I saw the Dowager frequently, more often with Sigurd or Philip than alone. At first I expected to meet one or other of the people she would mention, until I understood they belonged to a past she would not willingly relinquish. Even then I suspected that in many of her tales the same individuals appeared under different names and guises and I came to wonder how much she told me was true. Although I dropped hints to this effect, I had not the heart to challenge her and listened patiently as the stories were repeated.

Philip's invitation had brought me to London with the hope rather than expectation of a romantic affair. After the euphoria of my arrival had worn off, his pettiness and moods began to irritate and it was not long before I began to explore the capital's attraction's on my own. He accused me of being ungrateful, which I was not; I had promised him nothing and felt no responsibility for his self-deception. His jealousy did not impress me and as I became more successful and saw him embedded in his rut, my respect gradually died.

The Dowager saw us quarrelling and willed us to stop. As the younger partner, I was expected to make allowances, but being the younger partner I could not. Disapproving, and probably disliking me, she was nevertheless incapable of rejecting me, for I was the last of her young friends.

"You've made me very sad," she said, almost the last time we met. "I had so hoped that you and Philip would get on. You seemed perfectly suited. And now you tell me you're moving out to a place of your own. You'll regret it, I know."

For once her natural dignity had given way and she teetered between tears and anger. If I felt remorse, it was for her, not Philip.

"It's for the best," I said.

"No, it isn't." For the first time she raised her voice. "You'll be on your own and that's a terrible thing."

At that moment, to be on my own sounded like the sweetest of all blessings.

I intended to visit the Dowager once I had moved into my new home, but I had little time and, consciously or not, wished to sever all contact with Philip. Once, a year or two later, on my way to a friend's house, I found myself walking along her street. I should go down, I knew, but I merely walked slower as I passed, glancing over the railing and seeing the entrance even more neglected than before.

Every few months Philip and I would see each other in a theatre or a bar, but pride prevented us from saying hello. At first I took perverse pleasure in seeing how haggard he looked and how often he glanced in my direction; later I learnt that another young man, more pliable or loyal, had taken my place. I, meanwhile, let my emotions wander. Only after several years did I consider myself ready to settle down and only then was I willing to speak to Philip again.

The conversation started stiffly, but relaxed as we recognised neither had anything to fear from the other. He was very happy at the moment, for a second novel he had written had been accepted. Sigurd still drank and sold no paintings. The Dowager, poor dear, was in a home. A terrible place, he had heard. He could not visit her, for such places made him ill.

It was not guilt that made me drive out to see her, but a genuine desire to meet an old friend. She sat upright in the corner of a dayroom where other inmates sat dozing or gabbling to the empty air. She was thinner than I had remembered and the lack of make-up was almost an insult.

"Hello, Dowager," I said as cheerfully as possible. "It's me, Paul. Do you remember?"

She studied me carefully. The aristocratic airs had become a parody of age.

"I used to live with Philip. The writer."

"Ah yes," she said, obviously unable to recall.

"I visited you often, with Philip and Sigurd."

She suddenly smiled. "You painted my picture. I've got it in my room. Everyone admires it." Her words were slow; I wondered if she were drugged.

"I didn't paint it, Dowager. I... I lived with Philip. I came from Huddersfield."

"I've never been to Huddersfield."

"No, not you. Me." There was no recollection. I persevered a little more then turned to other matters — how she enjoyed the home, what she had done that day, what there would be for tea. She showed no more interest. Eventually I could stand it no longer and stood up to leave. It was then she woke up, told me how glad she had been to see me and asked if I could not stay.

"I must go, Dowager, I'm afraid, but I will come back to see you. Next week, if I can."

The glazed look returned. The old lady whom I had once respected as a source of wisdom and knowledge was now pathetic. I leant over and, for the first time, kissed her.

Business took me out of the country for over a month. I hurried back to her, small souvenirs of my travels in hand. It was too late; she had died in her sleep ten days before.

THE COMING
OF
SANTA CLAUS

"Is Santa Claus gay?" Peter mused aloud as he carefully draped the last strand of tinsel over the lower branches of the Christmas tree.

"I don't think so," said Terry, inspecting the leather-clad fairy that was precariously perched on the uppermost branch. "There's a Mrs Claus."

"That doesn't mean anything. Anyway, how do you know?"

"She appeared in *Santa Claus Meets the Martians on Broadway* or its sequel; I'm not sure which. It was on TV a few years ago."

"Be serious," Peter said. "I'm talking about real life."

"What do you mean, 'real life'? Santa Claus doesn't exist. And if he did and was gay, he'd hardly be the most desirable of men."

"Not in the classical sense, no," Peter conceded, standing back to admire their handiwork. "Looks nice, doesn't it? Much better than last year's."

"That's because your little brother isn't here to object to the angels."

"You can see his point. They don't usually fly around naked."

"Rather them than Santa Claus. Can you imagine making love with him?"

"Oh yes," Peter enthused. "Those kind eyes and that lovely

warm beard."

"That paunch and that dreadful laugh."

"All the more cuddly. Would you mind, really?"

"Would I mind what?" Terry asked, noting that pine needles were already beginning to litter the carpet.

"If I made love with Santa Claus."

"You're out of your mind. You know perfectly well there's no such person, so why should I care? As long as you didn't make it a habit."

"You know something, Terry? It's little things like your tolerance that make me love you."

With school closed for the holidays, Peter had two days to wander around the West End and do most of his Christmas shopping. The crowds were irritating, but by lunchtime on Friday he had bought nearly everything on his list. There only remained, to complement the deodorant, underwear and box of assorted razors he was going to give to Terry, a leather-bound edition of the complete works of the Marquis de Sade. Hatchards had been decidedly frosty on the subject, Harrods had suggested he try the toy department and the assistant in Foyles had had difficulty in understanding any European language. Resolving to try Bloomsbury in the afternoon, Peter dropped into the nearest gay pub and ordered himself a pie and a pint.

The bar was full of besuited gents made merry by the seasonal spirit, dubious youths liberally flashing ten-pound notes and moustachioed couples discussing which set of parents they would have to visit. Stomach satisfied, Peter pushed his empty plate to one side, downed a liberal draught of Very Peculiar and looked around. There was, he had decided, no one he knew, when a flash of red in the corner caught his eye. "It can't be," Peter thought, "but it is. It's Santa Claus!"

Indeed, at the far end of the bar, ignored by those around him and staring quietly into his beer, stood a rotund figure in a red suit and drooping bobble cap. Despite his full, almost artificial, white beard, he seemed much younger than Peter had imagined, yet there could be no doubt that it was Santa Claus.

Normally too shy to speak to strangers, Peter pushed his way through the crowded pub, afraid that someone else would get to him first. But the other customers seemed unaware of the celebrity in their midst and Peter was able to squeeze an arm onto the bar next to Santa, who disinterestedly turned to glance at his new neighbour.

"Hi," said Peter with unaccustomed confidence. "How're you? How're Donner and Blitzen?"

Santa looked surprised. "I'm sorry, mate, I don't speak German." He had a slight Cockney accent.

"Nor do I," Peter was confused. "I meant how are the reindeer? Rudolph, Donner, Blitzen and the others?"

"Oh, the reindeer." Santa knocked back his glass and signed for another. They're fine, just fine."

"I'm Peter."

"And I'm Santa Claus," he announced his name with unexpected vehemence.

"I'm surprised to see you here. Aren't you busy at the moment?"

"Yeah, well, I get a lunchbreak like every other worker."

"Do you come here often?" Peter asked. After all, Santa Claus or no Santa Claus, cruising still had its time-honoured routine.

"From time to time."

"You don't look very happy," Peter pointed out as Santa drained his glass again. "I expected a big grin and all ho-ho-ho. Or is that just for the kids?"

"We all have our worries. Like what I'm going to do after Christmas."

Santa straightened up as if to shake off that particular care. He really was, despite the frown, a fine figure of a man. There was even now a hint of that smile. If only . . . Peter thought. Well, why not? Terry had said that he wouldn't mind. Except Peter really ought to look for those books. On the other hand, a bottle of whisky would do just as well . . . "Er, Santa? Are you busy this afternoon? I mean, could the dwarves fill in for you?"

Santa examined his partner more closely. "They might. What did you have in mind?" Peter told him. Santa's grin became a wide smile. "Just let me make a phone call."

"To Mrs Claus?" Santa looked blank. "No, I suppose not."

As they rattled through the underground and two little children stared at his companion in amazement, Peter showed Santa each of the presents he had bought. Santa was particularly interested to hear about the leather-bound de Sade. It wasn't something he'd had much call for and to Peter's disappointment he couldn't suggest anywhere to buy it.

Once in bed, Santa's body proved to be young, lean and muscular, as well as surprisingly tanned for someone who spent most of the year at the North Pole. He made love energetically, his only inhibition being a sensitivity about his beard. Peter was allowed to stroke its silky softness but not to pull or run his fingers through it. Otherwise Peter could do as he wished and though the hour was spent in more athletics than cuddling, in no way was he disappointed.

When Santa left, after another beer "for the sleigh", Peter asked if they could see each other again. Santa looked uncertain. "Drop me a line."

"At the North Pole?"

Santa nodded. "You could send it express. Up the chimney."

Although he had enjoyed himself, there had been something odd about the whole business, Peter thought as he closed the door. As if Santa hadn't really been himself, but only pretending. Anyway, just think what Terry would say when he heard.

"You what? With whom?" Terry looked anything but pleased.

"Well, you said you wouldn't mind. And you're hardly innocent yourself."

"But I don't do it in our bed. And I don't pretend it's Santa bloody Claus."

"But it *was*."

"Peter, I'm beginning to doubt your sanity and to feel for the kids you teach. I'm sure they have more sense than you when it comes to Santa Claus. They'd probably mug him."

The atmosphere was seasonally frosty for the next two days, but by Christmas morning a thaw had set in. They sat in the living-room and opened their presents in turn. From Terry there was an expensive woollen jumper, a couple of records that Peter had searched for in vain and an attractive silver ring. In comparison, Peter's collection of small gifts seemed trivial and he sat glumly as Terry thanked him for each one. At last he came to a large parcel that Peter did not recognise.

"To Terry from Santa Claus," Terry read. "Very funny. What is it? A year's supply of condoms?"

Peter was about to protest, but his voice dried as Terry pulled off the wrapping. Inside was a fine leather-bound edition of the collected works of the Marquis de Sade.

IT WAS,
I SUPPOSE,
INEVITABLE

that I run into you. We live in a small town and there are only so many streets to walk along on a warm, sunny day. I had told myself that I was shopping, that I had foresaken papers I had to write and syllabuses I had to prepare in order to make way for the spring-cleaning I should have begun weeks before. It was an excuse, of course; all I wanted was an afternoon off, a few hours in which to do and think about nothing. So I was wandering down towards the river, enjoying the illusion of independence and freedom and the heightened awareness of colour and sound that comes at such moments, when I saw you.

I had no reason to avoid you — indeed I had had dinner with you and Ed the night before — but I did not want to speak to you just then. Even saying hello, passing some comment about the meal and walking on would have disturbed my mood, sent small unwelcome waves scurrying across the surface of my mind. I hesitated, you saw me, and it was too late to walk into the shop I was passing and pretend a sudden interest in a new washing-machine or a second television. So I returned your smile and watched you approach, a tall, dark-haired figure with an attractively lazy gait; I felt nothing and was not sure what I should feel.

We greeted each other with the warmth that either masks or

overrides all other emotion. You asked if I had enjoyed last night and I said I had, for the company had been pleasant and the food — your responsibility — as good as ever. "We didn't get much chance to talk," you said, part in regret and part in accusation. It was true, for I had been both reluctant to speak to you and happy to make in Linda a new acquaintance who shared some of my interests and appreciated my sense of humour. "You should come over one evening," you went on. "Ed and I never see you alone these days. All these dinner parties — it makes us feel like an old married couple."

I muttered something or shrugged my shoulders, wondering how soon I could get away from you and your domestic life and return to calm solitude, but, perhaps in acknowledgment of the days when we had been closer, you had to press the point, to ask whether I was busy at that moment. No, I said, seeing the trap yet unable to walk round it. "What about coffee?" I agreed, certain that the drink itself, the actions of raising and lowering the cup, of tinkering with the spoon, would be enough to absorb the tensions created by your presence. The Riverview was nearby; we walked towards it, talking about Linda. Ed had known her for years, you told me, since university; they still met as often as they could. As you talked, my mind wandered. For a brief moment I was conscious again of your good looks, noticed the first delicate lines of age; I felt a perverse pride in being with you and wondered if those who saw us, who thought about such things, would see us as a couple and envy us.

The Riverview was busy but not full, its tables taken by as many holidaymakers as residents. I saw and smiled at two of my students who were staying on for the summer. We sat down, a waitress appeared, took our order and went away. "We could be on the continent," I said, appreciating the opportunity to sit in the open air. Your response was some platitude that showed your thoughts were elsewhere. "No sign of a job?" I went on, trying to keep all false sympathy from my voice. You said no and I wondered how hard you had tried, whether you had forced yourself to apply for posts that would take you away from Ed, whether you were willing to do something other than teach.

"What will you do if nothing comes through?" I asked, allowing room for a miracle that would not occur. "Ed'll set me up in a restaurant." To me your certainty was false, for I had heard the story before, had been hearing it for over a year. Your lover's promise was your liferaft, your line to safety that could be hauled in when the gentle waves you were happy to drift through became breakers that threatened to overwhelm you, to drag you down. "When'll that be?" I asked, allowing you your dream. "Soon," you told me, "soon."

Neither of us spoke and I let my gaze rest on you, at the blue eyes that I had once taken for wisdom and now saw as naivety, at the scar across your forehead that had faded under your light tan, at the mouth which suggested reserve rather than your irrepressible honesty. You were four years older but no less attractive than the first time we had met, in that bar which I often visited but never ceased to resent. I walked in and saw you standing alone, looking, I was sure, for someone to sleep with. When I approached you, you told me you had a lover but would be happy to talk; a fool, I stayed, told myself that your words were only a gambit, that if not that night then the next you would weaken, allow yourself to be persuaded home to my bed.

"Are you busy?" you asked, breaking the silence. I nodded, mentioned the articles I was writing, department changes, preparations for the coming year. You showed interest although I am sure you felt none, asked what I was working on as if you both could and wanted to discuss it with me. Once I would have been flattered, excited by your questions, seen them as a prelude to greater intimacy; now I wondered if you hated the courtesy, if you envied or despised me, my work, my financial security. But I was being uncharitable; you have always cared about me, worried that in one way or another my life was not complete, even sought out lovers for me. Except that when it was you I wanted, or thought I wanted, you would not accede.

I mentioned Ed, forgetting or ignoring the fact that I had seen you both the day before. "He's fine," you said, and I went on to ask what I already knew, about the cases he had, about his plans to move out or set up on his own. You told me, and I noticed,

perhaps even listened for, the hollowness, the disguised disappointment in your answers, the sense that you knew about his
decisions but were not involved in them. Yet your words and
feelings outlined your lover as if he were with us; in recalling his
impatience, his stubbornness, his sharp wit, they cast an image
as three-dimensional and insubstantial as a hologram. I remembered that at first I had disliked him, not merely because he was
the wall that defended you from me, but because all his strengths
and virtues seemed negative, aggressive and cruel. Later I was
surprised to find myself enjoying his company, to see a friendship develop that encompassed you both. I envied Ed his
intimacy with you, you his intimacy with him, and for a while
even daydreamed that one day the three of us might live
together, might share some large, warm and almost mystic bed.

You did not know that, did you? You thought in your
innocence and generosity that my lust for you had died that first
night we met, that my motives for meeting you again were no
more than amicable. But my desires, my needs are stronger and
broader than yours; I am driven by more than deep affection.
For as long as you are attractive I will respond to that attraction,
even when, as now, our personalities have changed, our posi-
tions are reversed and I find myself, in unguarded moments,
pitying you.

Again the talk between us died and I sat looking over the river,
watching another coach crawl across the bridge, imagining its
guide telling her camera-carrying charges of the rustic splen-
dours of the Riverview Cafe. You ordered another coffee, asked
if I wanted one. I wondered what Ed was doing, what clients he
was seeing, what papers he was signing, what he would think of
the two of us together. It was perhaps not coincidence that you
mentioned him again. "Ed's thinking of going on holiday," you
said. "He doesn't want me to come." You raised your eyebrows,
pretending to make light of it, but all I saw was a little boy lost,
afraid he had done wrong. "Why?" I asked, the first thing that
came into my head. "I don't know." "I wouldn't worry about it,"
I tried, almost routinely, to reassure you. "You've been together
five years. There's nothing wrong in wanting some time alone."

"That's only part of it," you said. "There're other things."

I should have stopped you there, silenced you with a vague conciliatory remark and moved on to the weather or mutual friends. Even better, I should have looked at my watch, remembered an appointment, a phone call to make, a shop about to close, and left you more surprised at my behaviour than concerned about your lover. I was, however, curious, even felt in some way responsible, while you, having eased open the floodgates, were eager to drain all your emotions and frustrations. So I asked what you meant and you told me he had become offhand, that he had begun to lose his temper with you, that there were times when you felt there was nothing you could do right. I listened, helpless, my sympathy both hypocritical and sincere. "Have you talked to him about it?" I asked and you said you had, that there had been a long conversation a few nights before. Ed, apparently, had apologised for his behaviour, had claimed it was the pressure of work, but you were not sure that you believed him, you were afraid the two of you were drifting apart.

As I sat there, trying to disentangle the truth from your vision of it, to unite your words with what I already knew, I imagined the two of you together, in your living-room with the walls a comfortable shade of green and the furniture too carefully positioned, or in bed, sitting side by side with the covers up to your navels as in a vaguely risqué comedy scene. I could hear your reasonableness and Ed's impatience, I could see the slight frown crinkling your scar and the wide-eyed expression Ed adopts when he is pretending a situation does not make him uncomfortable. I could even hear the tones you both used — your fear that Ed might no longer want you overlain by your urge to be rational and fair, to do whatever was right, Ed's exasperation hidden by a guilt which in turn had to be masked. You tried not to plead, he tried not to scold. I recognised and was angered by the extent of your weakness, by your inability to create a life of your own, yet at the same time I felt for you, for I knew your virtues lay elsewhere — in your loyalty, your warmth and generosity.

"Maybe you can talk to him," you said. But I have, I almost told you, I have. "What would I say?" I asked. "Just try and find out what's wrong." But I already knew what was wrong and I regretted even more that I had not left you when I had the chance, regretted that I was forced to sit and talk, to hide my exasperation and self-satisfaction, when I would rather be a mile, ten miles, a thousand miles away. "I don't see the point," I said. "Why should he tell me anything he won't tell you?" "Perhaps he's afraid to talk to me. And he likes you." How naive you are, I thought, what straws you are clutching at, to imagine that mere liking is enough. If I did not already know what was happening and know so much more than you, Ed would never tell me, no matter how much he liked me, how carefully, how subtly I inquired. He never confides in people, never tells them any more than he wants them to know.

You were looking at me, waiting for the answer which I did not have. For a moment I felt like a solicitor approached by both parties in a divorce and having to choose which one to represent. The fact that for almost three months I had been making love with Ed, enjoying his humour and his company in those rare moments when neither you nor work claimed his time, was irrelevant; you were both my friends and I did not wish to hurt either of you. "I might say something," I said, "but I'm not going to insist. I'm not a marriage guidance counsellor." I smiled but you were not amused. "Could you?" you said. "Why don't you go out with him, take him for a drink?" Again I almost spoke, pointed out the irony of the cuckold pushing the lover towards his wife's bed. "If you really want me to . . ." My reluctance was not feigned; I was already deceiving you on one level and did not want to deceive you on two. "Look," I interrupted whatever you were going to say, "leave it for a week or so, see how things go on. You might discover everything is all right, there is nothing to worry about." And in that week, that fortnight, I too might discover Ed's intentions, might worm my way past his careful comments and unyielding compromises, might force him as delicately and stubbornly as he forces his clients, to finally leave either you or me.

Your relief was sudden and visible, as if all I had to do was talk to Ed briefly, point out where he had gone wrong and how everything could be put right. I felt for a moment irritation, both that you expected me to heal your wound and that you could be so naive as to believe that I could, but that emotion was swept aside by a sudden helplessness, by the awareness that whether Ed stayed with you or came to me depended on neither of us, on nothing you or I could say or do. Only a few hours earlier, in the snack bar where Ed and I often met, I had heard about your conversation of two nights before and seen it as my cue, my opportunity to ask what he was going to do, when he was going to tell you about me. My courage, however, failed me; I was defeated by the fear that he might say now was not the time, that there never would be a time. So I said nothing, talked only about work in the few minutes until he had to leave, and found myself going home, where I tried to concentrate on papers and was unable to do so.

You said something and I had to ask you to repeat it. Relieved of your burden, you were telling me about your new neighbours, the pleasant mother and the precocious child. I made some comment and you talked on, oblivious of the fact that I was now as distracted as you had been, that my mind was focused on the problem that for you was solved. As I nodded and grunted at the appropriate moments I thought about Ed, tried to understand how I had fallen in love with him, how the initial irreverence, the attraction that was no more than physical had given way to the need to see and be with him. It was, I suppose, when he allowed me to glimpse his dissatisfaction with you, when I understood that to him your qualities were defects, that, hardly aware of what I was doing, I began to compare myself with you as his lover. I was convinced that you had become no more than a habit for him, that whatever had been your attraction had long since been diluted by familiarity, while it was I who now possessed what he admired — a career, self-assurance, distrust of others. Further-more, I was my own master, neither needed nor demanded his presence twenty-four hours in every day. It was only logical that in time he would leave you, transfer his allegiance to me and let you fade from our lives as a friend who was occasionally seen and more often pitied.

All that, I now realise, was illusion, as great an illusion as your imagining that I only needed to say a few words to Ed and he would return the affectionate lover he had once been. In sitting and talking with me you had been neither a rival nor a friend but a mirror in which I had seen myself, a mirror in which your presence rather than your words, your emotions rather than your appearance, had revealed to me the person I was unwittingly becoming. The impression of self-confidence and strength that I maintained from the days when it had been substance might still deceive you and the rest of the world, but the more I wanted Ed, the sooner I would find myself as dependent on him as you were, as you had always been. It was ironic, I thought, that the greater my desire for Ed the less I would be the person he wanted me to be, while to be that person would mean that I no longer desired him. All I had achieved in three months was to deceive myself as completely as I had been deceiving you.

At last my inattention compelled you to say you had to go. You stood up, dropped money onto the table and thanked me sincerely for my patience and time. I watched you walk out into the street, suspecting you were going to see Ed, for he had told me that you often dropped by in the afternoon. I imagined you would tell him you had seen me, might even repeat the suggestion he have a drink with me. He would listen, agree to please you, his solemn expression masking his amusement. Shortly, however, he would say that it had been good to see you but he had work to do and, graciously dismissed like a subject by his sovereign, you would apologise for disturbing him and leave. As you closed the door, his head would be already bent to study contracts and you and I would be as absent from his thoughts as if we did not exist. Perhaps indeed for him neither of us did.

I sat in the afternoon warmth surrounded by the monotone of overlain conversations and the fragments of my complacency, wondering if I still had the choice of forgetting Ed, of telling him the game was over, that our meetings would have to stop because — the excuse was easy and in character — I was getting bored. If I were to do so it would not be for your sake but for mine, for fear of what would happen when I could no longer control my feelings, for fear, in short, that I might become like you. Yet my reluctance to take that step, to cut him off, told me that it was perhaps already too late, that my emotions had, without my knowledge, escaped my control. For the first time in many years I wanted to make a decision and could not. I could only sit back with my eyes closed against the sun and wait, hope that a shadow would fall across them. Then I would look up and see you or Ed telling me what was going to happen, what I must do. It was a warm day and long afternoon; with any luck one of you would come.

GANYMEDE

It was Sergio who told Renato about the many foreigners in Rio, those who had made it their home and those who only came to spend three or four weeks on a wild and riotous holiday. They were tall, blond and attractive men who liked to laugh and drink and who could spend more money in an evening than either Sergio or Renato earned in a month. Those who liked boys could be found on the beach in front of the big white Copacabana Palace Hotel by day and at the pavement tables of the Galeria Alaska by night. When they took a fancy to a young Brazilian they would give him presents of money and jewellery and clothes. And occasionally a gringo would fall so much in love that he would take his new friend back to Europe or the United States and the two of them would live happily together like brothers or like father and son.

In the seventeen years of his life Renato had seldom left the small town in the heart of Brazil where he had been born and only once, as a young child, had he been taken to Rio and seen the sea. He knew every flake of paint on every shabby house in every dusty street of his birthplace, which he loathed with the same intensity as he loathed the youths who loitered noisily in the town's bars and the girls who giggled together on their evening walks. Growing out of childhood, he had come to see his surroundings and acquaintances as a poor and cruel substitute for the expensively furnished apartments and handsomely dressed men and women who appeared each night on the soap operas he watched avidly on the family's old and unreliable television.

Far removed from Renato's hot and dusty world, not only were the lives portrayed richer, but the loves, angers and griefs were surely deeper and purer than the emotions that surrounded him — his sisters' petty infatuations, his father's brief rages and his own impotent unhappiness. Sergio's words, therefore, were no more than a detail to be added to a picture he was already familiar with, confirmation that indeed in Rio he too would be at home.

From the age of fourteen Renato had worked in the family shop until business slackened with the opening of the new supermarket three blocks away. Since then he had worked for *seu* Carlos, the owner of the only clothes shop in town. His brothers, who worked in a garage repairing farm machinery, were better paid, but they came home at the end of each day tired and covered in grease and oil, whereas he was surrounded by bright colours and cloths of every description. On the few occasions that *seu* Carlos left him in charge, Renato would rummage through the racks and drawers, trying on different trousers, shirts, even dresses, then swirl around in them in front of the mirror, let the fresh, clean texture rub against his skin and imagine himself in the streets, the apartments and the best restaurants in Rio.

His father and brothers accused him of being lazy and soft; he had learnt to ignore them as he ignored his sisters' mocking and his mother's daily complaints about her illnesses and her life. Their presence was no more disturbing than the mosquitoes which continually buzzed but only occasionally settled to bite. The neighbours were no different, other large families whose days were dominated by work and gossip and whose evenings were spent in the local bar or around the television screen. The youths he had grown up with paid him little attention, except to jeer at him during the day or, late at night, to cajole him into relieving their urgent desires with more efficiency and less protest than the girlfriends they claimed to have.

The only person he called his friend was Sergio, an older boy who, years before, had first pointed out the two bars where long-distance drivers from out of town were to be found. They had grown slowly apart, but still shared confidences until the day that Sergio packed a small suitcase and waited one long, hot after-noon for the bus to take him to Rio and the wealth and freedom each had promised himself. Weeks later, Sergio returned for a brief visit to entrance Renato with tales of a dream come true, of streets where shop after shop sold nothing but the most beauti-ful clothes, where the beaches stretched as far as the eye could see, and where discos and bars played the latest music all night and men kissed and danced together for all the world to see. Young men like Renato could earn thousands of cruzados working as models or acting in television shows and if he was not lucky, there were the gringos who could make reality of his dreams. And no, it did not matter that he came from the interior, for the gringos were afraid that all the boys from the city had Aids.

Within a week Renato had left home, in his back pocket some money stolen from *seu* Carlos' till. Neither his parents nor his brothers showed surprise or regret at his going, only his very youngest sister, when she understood what was happening, began to cry. On the short walk to the bus station, as he passed the tired houses sagging in the summer sun, his chest seized with a new emotion, one that was both relief and apprehension. Looking out of the bus window, waiting for it to depart, he looked at the men, middle-aged, old, unshaven and tired, who sat talking at the open-air bar. Only this bus, it seemed to Renato, the one clear thought in his mind, saved him from one day joining them.

His image of Rio was a city of tall white apartment blocks overlooking golden sands and the blue ocean. He was not prepared for the long approach through grimy outer suburbs, where, on either side of an eight-lane avenue clogged with traffic belching fumes, mile after mile of shanty-towns eventually gave way to grey warehouses, giant billboards and fast-food restau-rants. The men and women he saw queuing at bus-stops looked as poor as those he had left behind, only more anxious and more pressed for time. From the bus station it was many enquiries and a long journey under skies dark with rain to the narrow, dirty street which Sergio had given as his address. On the top floor the door opened off a dark anonymous hall to a small and featureless room and only Sergio's welcome and the realisation that he had at last left home prevented Renato from bursting into tears of exhaustion and disappointment.

A long sleep, a day of rest and the following evening in the streets and bars of Copacabana restored the promise of expectations fulfillled. Men and women in bright fashionable clothes sparkled around the tables of the outdoor cafes, sipping unfamiliar drinks, eating exotic food, talking with words that Renato understood but whose meaning was beyond his comprehension. In a discotheque the thick beat of the music, the darkness and flashing lights created a magic in which fairy-tales came true and all men became lovers; outside again, the broad sweep of the Avenida, with the ocean in darkness facing the serried ranks of the tall floodlit buildings standing shoulder to shoulder, was the proof Renato had sought that the Rio he had dreamt of did indeed exist and that he at last had found his home.

The next day was a Saturday, and, sitting on the sands with Sergio, he found himself surrounded by near-naked light-footed and light-voiced youths of his age and men of more ponderous smiles and tones. Some glanced at him with curiosity, others with the universal expression of invitation. Sergio greeted a few friends, but made it clear to Renato that he came here less and less frequently, preferring those parts of the city where the Brazilians were more masculine and foreigners were rare. It was, however, the foreigners who attracted Renato most, the men in their thirties, forties and fifties easily identified by their garbled Portuguese, their height and the pallor or golden tone of their skin. They had a quality he could sense but barely discern, far less understand, a mystery which his compatriots, whether young or old, lacked. He waited for one of them to turn his way and speak and, when none did, fended off his disappointment with the promise of many such days to come, with all the opportunities they would bring.

Difficulties, however, presented themselves before any such opportunities. Within a few days came the realisation that the money he had expected to last him several weeks had almost gone. Sergio had taken much of it to pay for food and rent, while the rest disappeared on bus-trips, a swimming costume and each night's drinks. At home, poverty had been as natural as breathing, but here Renato knew that without money he could not survive. No longer were a roof over his head and a solid meal every evening assured, while the new clothes and transistor radio he had promised himself became as remote as the cars and colour televisions displayed in the same shops. And if he wanted to stay with him more than a few days, Sergio now insisted, they must move to a bigger place, with all the additional expenditure that implied.

Renato had dreamt of being a model but had no idea where to begin. The stories Sergio had told of magazine covers and television roles dwindled under questioning to anecdotes based on chance encounters rather than universal plan. Telling himself it was only temporary, he took a job in the same furnishing chain where Sergio worked, travelling each day to a different branch to unload beds, chairs and tables with other youths who, with no ill feeling, happily mocked his country accent and ignorance. It was, he realised, preferable to begging and in time he even began to enjoy the work and banter, but his mind was constantly elsewhere — on the next day at the beach or the previous night in the bars, the man he had been introduced to or hoped to meet, the riches he had seen but not yet gained.

It was not difficult to make acquaintances among the youths who loitered on the beach or the streets of Copacabana and from them he soon learnt the informal hierarchy and customs of the world he had joined. A few, he recognised, had money and no need of patronage, but most, like himself, were seeking a path out of poverty. Some saw each new encounter as a means of immediate income, but others were more patient, believing with Renato that where affection began, greater wealth would surely follow. Of course he knew that some Brazilian men were as wealthy as gringos, but they were seldom generous, whereas all foreigners, because they had travelled so far, had to be rich and few were unwilling to spend money on others. The pattern was well-established; first the potential companion would be bought a drink or two and perhaps the entry to a disco. If all went well, a meal would follow, or a trip up the Sugar Loaf; as affection grew, there would be presents and a little spending money. In time, for those who were lucky, there was the trip to Europe or North America and, if all went well, the symbols of total commitment: a residence permit, a bank account, sometimes — although Renato was not sure how they worked — a credit card. There were even stories of boys being paid to go to college and given cars of their own. And all the gringos wanted in return were the only things that Renato could give: his time, his love and his complete devotion.

At first with foreigners Renato was tongue-tied, afraid to speak and reveal his ignorance of the ways of the world. It was a relief to understand that most did not care that his English was confined to the words and phrases he had picked up on the bars and beach, that he had forgotten his schooling, that he confused cities and countries, that he knew nothing of politics or presidents. His new friends had come to Rio for physical pleasure, not intellectual stimulation; they expected him only to laugh and smile, to know little more than which drink to order and which discotheque to visit. Relaxed in their company, Renato could and did enjoy himself, accepted their drinks, laughed with them, danced when the opportunity arose. But for reasons he did not understand, the invitations to dinner alone, to a day visiting the resorts of Petropolis or Cabo Frio did not come and the intimacy of hotel or apartment bedrooms soon dissolved in the harsh sunlight of the beach or at the pavement table of a bar.

His expectations, although not his hopes, had nearly died when, on a cloudy day with the beach near deserted, he met a North American who lived in São Paulo. In his thirties, with dark, curly hair, attractive eyes, a well-maintained body and good, if accented, Portuguese, John offered Renato the single-minded attention denied him by others. In return, Renato abandoned his work, Sergio and friends. For ten days he succumbed to John's demands like a tame dog to its master; in bars and restaurants he listened and nodded, only half-understanding, as John opinionated on films and books or explained to foreign and Brazilian friends alike the deficiencies in the national character that kept his adopted country in eternal chaos. When Renato's attention wandered, it was to congratulate himself on his handsome lover and to hope that acquaintances who saw him envied his status. He began to plan and wonder about his life in São Paulo, only realising on the last day of John's visit that John neither wanted nor intended to see him again.

Deep unhappiness turned to anger and a resolve never to find himself in such a situation again. The image of John in his mind, which had once made his heart swell with happiness, now made it shrink with hatred. All foreigners might not be as dishonest, but with their smiles and bonhomie he could not tell them apart; henceforth he would approach each as John had approached him — with open desire and hidden contempt. His anger was compounded by the situation he now found himself in; he had lost his job and it was a frightening, moneyless fortnight until he found another. His friendship with Sergio, who now worked in an office and was becoming a distant, humourless individual, had weakened and they had little to say to each other. At the worst moment of his depression he considered going home, but he would rather join the beggars on the streets than admit to his family that he could not survive without them. Even if they were to make him welcome and *seu* Carlos, by some miracle, took him back and made him manager of his shop, Renato knew that after Rio life in the small town would be unbearably ugly, petty and cruel.

Not that the experience with John reconciled Renato to the city; aspects of Rio that he had always disliked he now began to despise — the shanty-towns clinging to every hillface, the urchins that slept in the streets, the violence and crime. At the back of his mind he knew that the poverty he now had contempt for was the poverty from which he came, but this awareness increased rather than reduced the depth of his emotion. A latent racism emerged and he regarded with distaste the blacks and mulattos who crowded the buses and beaches and street where he lived, ignorant of the faint but attractive traces of negro ancestry in his own features. In North America, it seemed, there were many blacks and that rumour and the memory of John made him turn towards Europe as his goal. He met in quick succession a Frenchman and German who each tried to develop a close relationship, but their relative youth made them less wealthy and hence inconsequential in Renato's eyes and he took delight in disappointing them. It was only several weeks later, with Joseph, an old, unattractive Englishman, that he once more made an effort to be reliable.

They had met on the beach shortly before Carnival. It was Joseph's first visit to Brazil and conversation was slow, with many misunderstandings and references to the Englishman's phrase-book. When Joseph offered first a drink and then a meal, Renato hesitated, but it was a day of poor weather and there was no one else around he would rather speak to. As the afternoon shaded into evening and the meal was followed by a visit to Joseph's hotel room, Renato sought and heard the indications of wealth that he longed for — the large house, the car, the business that Joseph owned. There were drawbacks — Joseph was thin, wrinkled, pale and bespectacled and conversation was painfully slow and dry — but he was friendly and, unlike John, appeared to be undemanding both in and out of bed.

The next day, therefore, Renato saw no reason not to keep his appointment with Joseph. The strong light of a sunny day emphasised the Englishman's ugliness and Renato was on the point of inventing a soon-to-arrive German lover when Joseph asked if he would be his companion for the rest of his holiday. All expenses would be met, of course, and, allowing for the difficulties of translation, there were hints of gifts that the youth might expect. For the briefest moment Renato thought of work — the drudgery and minimum wage of the snack bar where he had already skipped several days — and happily agreed.

The three weeks which followed passed more easily than Renato had anticipated. Joseph was a quiet person who pre-ferred to remain silent than to force a message across the language barrier between them, while Renato was not expected

to always entertain. They sat on the beach or in bars and watched
the crowds, talking to some and listening to others, or, Joseph's
guidebook in hand, explored baroque churches or dusty museums that Renato had not even known existed. There he would
follow Joseph silently, more awed than bored, unable to place
these tall, dark, cool, silent buildings in the image he had created
for himself of Brazil. And there were times when they sat and
talked and Joseph told him about his business importing flowers, his marriage years ago and his daughter. In turn, Renato told
him about his family, but there was little enthusiasm in his voice
and Joseph soon learnt that it was the present and future which
interested the youth rather than the past.

There were frustrations with Joseph. Although he would not
refuse a shirt or pair of shoes that Renato admired, he did not
offer money for the difficult times that the boy knew lay ahead.
Sex between them remained unadventurous and, despite his
experience with John, Renato sometimes longed for the younger,
stronger and more handsome foreigners who had arrived in Rio
for Carnival. In discotheques, where Joseph occasionally allowed himself to be taken, Renato had to dance alone, unable to
persuade the old man to join the mass of jerking bodies on the
floor. And, although it was a problem too vague for Renato to
identify, there was no closeness between them, no way in which
he could explain to Joseph the emotions that sometimes flooded
his mind, the unhappiness, the doubts, the occasional joy that
made up his life.

He had not expected that Joseph would invite him back to
London. He had pretended no affection and it had not occurred
to him that someone with whom he was not in love and who did
not appear to love him would make such an offer. Both as-
tounded and suspicious, he said yes, expecting the Englishman
to change his mind, and it was not until he saw the air ticket made
out in his name and Joseph delayed his own departure to
complete the formalities for Renato's passport that the Brazilian
allowed himself to believe that the dream was coming true.

He left for London with the same hope and dread that he had
left his birthplace. Many of those he said goodbye to would, he

was sure, forget him within the week; he was sad to leave them more because they were the only people he knew than for any friendship they had offered him. Sergio wished him well, but there was no envy in his voice; they promised to write, but Renato doubted that either would. To his parents he sent a short letter that had taken hours to write, hoping they were well and giving Joseph's address. He had wanted to say more, but the blank page had stared at him and nothing came to mind.

In the taxi to the airport Joseph told him the story of Ganymede, a boy so beautiful that God had sent down a large bird to take him up to Heaven. He, Renato, was Ganymede, and if it was difficult to imagine Joseph as God, the enormous airplane was certainly the bird lifting him up into the skies. Unable to sleep during the long flight through the darkness, he sat nervous lest any word or action of his transgress some etiquette of which he was unaware. At last, after a long descent through thick cloud, he peered through the narrow window down at clusters of houses and patches of grass. As they came lower and he could distinguish cars on the roads, the fact that they were driving on the left rather than the right was final proof that this was all real, that he was indeed arriving in this strange exotic land.

The immigration officer was curious, but satisfied by Renato's return ticket, money and letter from Joseph. No customs official looked at their cases and shortly they were outside the crowded terminal and waiting for a taxi. Cold in his thin jacket and shirt and suddenly tired, Renato felt a few drops of rain and looked up at the grey skies, a reminder of unhappy times in Brazil. When their taxi arrived and he saw that the driver was black, he thought that somehow they had got on the wrong plane and arrived in New York, but no, Joseph laughed, this was London indeed.

Ganymede's spirits rose again on the long ride to Joseph's house, for there were no signs of poverty in the buildings and people that they passed. Nor was his new home a disappointment, for the large detached house, separated from the road by a generous garden, boasting its own garage and porticoed entrance, was grander than any building he had seen in Rio.

Inside, the thick carpets and curtains, the furniture and paintings, the books and ornaments crowding every table and shelf,
made him think he had entered a king's palace or a museum.
When he saw the size and comfort of the room that was to be his
alone, he turned in joy to Joseph and, to the other's surprise and
satisfaction, put his arms around him and gave him a kiss.

The nervousness of the first few days, surrounded by valuables both old and new that he dared not touch, dissolved into
warm pleasure as he became accustomed to living in such luxury.
When Joseph was at work he would wander round the house
carefully picking up and examining ornaments or wondering
how to work this or that machine — whether a dishwasher or a
fax, he could never quite understand Joseph's explanation.
There were three colour televisions and, although he understood little, he was happy to spend hours watching one or other
screen, especially cartoons, detective series and other pro-
grammes with more action than dialogue. At weekends the
streets and shops nearby became familiar and he welcomed the
opportunity to leave Joseph in the kitchen or the living-room so
he could go out and buy milk or a newspaper or whatever it was
that had been forgotten.

As time passed they settled into a routine whereby Joseph
would leave the house early and return in the early evening.
Renato would spend the morning in the house, in theory tidying
up, but in practice often leaving the breakfast dishes unwashed
until reminded. After lunch he would take the bus to the local
college where, in a class of Italian and Spanish au pair girls and
Arab restaurant workers, he tried to learn English without
admitting that he could barely write and read his own language.
The evenings were quiet, spent watching television or in conversations that faded a little more with each reference to the
dictionary. At weekends they would visit Joseph's friends, Renato sitting politely, soon giving up the effort of understanding
what was being said to let his mind follow patterns of wallpaper
or watch passers-by in the street. Once or twice a week there
would be guests to dinner or they would be others' guests. Most
of those Renato met were of Joseph's generation while those

who were younger, a Chinese boy, an effeminate white youth, would talk to him for a while but spend most of the evening in conversation with others.

In Rio Renato would have gone to the beach, where each day it had seemed he had met old friends and made new ones. In London there was no beach, it was the end of winter and the days were grey, damp and cold. In Rio he would have visited a disco or bar every night; in London Joseph was tired and would not let him go out alone. Discouraged by the English class, he started to explore the neighbourhood instead, walking along tree-lined avenues with grand but anonymous houses that seemed at once both unreal and forbidding. Or he would loiter in the shopping mall he had discovered, seeing the clothes, gadgets and records that he wanted to buy but which he knew Joseph would refuse. At home, on dull, wet days when there was nowhere to go and nothing to do, he wandered from room to room, picking up and fidgeting with the ornaments that only a few weeks before he had carefully avoided. There was a telephone, but no one to ring, except once when he had discovered the code for Brazil and dialled Sergio at his work before slamming down the receiver in fear of admitting his loneliness and failure.

More than once he suggested helping Joseph in his office, pointing out that he would not only be providing free labour but improving his English at the same time. At first Joseph laughed off the idea, later becoming annoyed when Renato persisted. That was not why he had brought the Brazilian to England; besides, his private life and business life were separate and as long as he worked it would remain so. Then give me money to do something, the youth almost pleaded. Do what? Joseph wanted to know, and when Renato could think of no reply, pointed out that he was already receiving bed, board, clothes and a small allowance each week. Defeated, Renato fell silent.

The greyness that had replaced gratitude in its turn became anger. In Rio Joseph had been kind, generous and always pleasant; in London each time he spoke it seemed to be an order or prohibition, in tones that often strayed into irritation. Renato gradually understood, without being able to put it into words, that Joseph had not brought a lover to England, but a status symbol, a pretty young Brazilian to be displayed to friends. It was a role Renato could accept, would voluntarily play, but on terms that allowed him his freedom. Joseph, however, offered no choice; he had given Renato much more than he had any right to expect and he must find his happiness at home.

The underground, at first a mystery, became a means of escape. It took him to the centre of the city, at first to places he had visited when sightseeing with Joseph, later to the bars he discovered by following identifiably gay men. Unsure of the customs, he loitered in corners until the scene became as familiar to him as their counterparts in Rio. He was often approached, offered drinks, time in bed. But when he told his new acquaintances how he had arrived in London, the problems he had and his unhappiness with Joseph, they nodded sympathetically and drifted away.

When Joseph learnt how Renato was spending his afternoons he refused to give him more money. If I can't do anything in London, I want to go back to Rio, give me my return ticket. But the ticket had only existed to deceive the immigration officer and Joseph had long since cashed it in. *Filha-da-puta, cagão!* Renato screamed in anger as he raised a fist to punch the older man. But Joseph was quicker and the sudden violence of the slap across the youth's face shocked both of them into remorse, mutual apologies and a few days where each was more considerate to the other.

A week later, however, in need of money, Renato took some silver cutlery to try to sell to a jeweller. The shopkeeper, suspicious, called the police, who eventually contacted Joseph. Furious, afraid of the scandal that might emerge, he confirmed Renato's story. At home they traded insults that were only partly understood; in frustration Renato picked up a vase and threw it against a wall. Then you can go home, Joseph said, if that's what you really want. I'll buy you a ticket and you can go next week. That night Renato lay in bed and thought of Rio, the long hours he had worked in the snack bar, the dirty grey room he had shared with Sergio, where the window was always open to the noise and exhaust of traffic, the days he had spent on the beach waiting for the rich young lover who had never come. He could not go back; despite the cold, wet weather, the loneliness, the frustrations of living with Joseph, here at least he had more than he had ever had in Brazil.

In Joseph's eyes, however, Renato's decision to stay implied acceptance of Joseph's terms. There would be no more visits to central London; he would return to his English classes and when he had passed his exams there would be others he could take that would give him a career. He would control his temper, learn to accept English manners, entertain Joseph's friends. Renato listened, half-understanding, wishing to do well, yet knowing something was missing without knowing what it was. For a time he played the part intended to make Joseph happy, but difficulties at college and lack of warmth at home sowed a seed of despair that over weeks grew into a deep weight of unhappiness. The day that Joseph once again refused to take him out in the evening, Renato stuffed some clothes into a bag, searched through the house for whatever money he could find and made his way to the city centre.

He had no clear idea of what he wanted to do. It was soon obvious that the money he had would not pay for even one night in a hotel. As the afternoon wore into evening he moved from bar to bar in search of the man who would take him in. His anxiety, however, prevented approaches and it was only chance which started him talking to a youth who had more than once been in a similar situation. There were discos he could enter cheaply, streets where he could stand and wait, but even guided by such knowledge, it was not until the early morning that he found himself in some middle-aged man's shabby bedroom. Told to leave as dawn was breaking, tired from lack of sleep, he found himself in a suburb he did not recognise. A cafe was open and he bought coffee and breakfast, served by a gross woman who took pleasure in misunderstanding his English. He sat at the window watching as it began to rain and passers-by ran for cover or put up their umbrellas. How long was it since he had seen the sun or felt its warmth? For the first time he was nostalgic for Rio.

In his pocket there was less than five pounds. He could not survive another day in London. Shortly he would telephone Joseph and he prayed that Joseph would take him back. He did not know whether that or wandering the streets was worse. He looked out at the rain again, despair welling up in him like a flooding river. With loud, uncontrolled sobs, Ganymede began to cry.

TRIANGLE

The telephone rings. "Jack? I'll be home late. Don't bother cooking for me." Jack puts down the receiver, the pain returning like the dull weight of a forgotten toothache. He stares at the wall and sees the evening stretching before him like a long road across the desert.

Michael steps out of the phone booth into a warm evening in late spring, the light slanting across the city making clothes brighter and faces more alive. He hungers to meet strangers, to talk and to flirt.

David returns to a house that has always been lifeless, where the dark brown walls of the hall lean inwards and only a weak light sifts through the glass door. The acrid smell of cats and gas is stronger — time, he recognises wearily, to clean again.

The self-pity will pass. Shortly Jack will get up, prepare a meal and settle to watch television, but at this moment Michael is his life and without Michael any action, any thought, is meaningless.

The fault is his own, he knows. In the year they have lived together Michael has never suggested that his friendship might dissolve into love, that the few nights they have slept together meant anything more than the other small favours they have done for each other. Jack, however, has fallen for Michael like an animal into a trap. He is incapable of not loving, finds Michael so warm and bright that he rushes towards him as a puppy breaks away to greet its master.

The bar is full. Two married couples on the way to the theatre talk over gin and wine, unaware, it appears, of the glances, conversation and dress of the men around them. Michael struggles through, eyes searching for old friends to greet, new friends to be made. At a corner of the bar he buys a drink and waits.

Dear Jack, sitting at home as patiently as an old and sleepy pet. He, Michael, should move, find another household, with more or younger flatmates. But he is comfortable with Jack, except on the days when the infatuation surfaces between them. Then Michael must behave as cautiously and courteously as royalty, knowing that his words and actions are saturated with meanings that he can neither guess nor withhold.

David is restless, keen to go out and yet afraid to do so. The familiar confusion tightens his stomach and dries his mouth. It would be better to stay at home and watch television with the cats, stroking and talking to them, listening to them purr. He knows, however, that shortly he will go back into town and force himself to talk and smile until, heart pumping and mind spinning, he persuades some young man to come back to this large and empty house where he is always alone.

This need, as always, brings Robin to mind and David remembers with strong and conflicting emotions the slim body, the round face and curly hair, the affection and the insults, the love-making and the violence. David cannot live without someone to take Robin's place and David knows that no one ever can.

In the kitchen Jack washes and cuts enough vegetables for two, performing each action with absent-minded efficiency. He thinks about calling someone, but there is no one to ring and nothing to say. He is not a gregarious person and finds it difficult to make friends, for he is unable to make small talk and unwilling to reveal what he really feels.

His thirtieth birthday approaches like the fall of night and he longs for a home and a lover with whom he can nestle for the gentle downward slope into age. Michael is not the one; there must be many others in the city who would return Jack's deep emotion, who seek rest rather than excitement. Yet none has Michael's smile, his sense of humour, his joy in life. So Jack can only wait and hope that one day his young friend will tire of flirting with the world and willingly return to be his partner.

Each man around Michael is a potential lover. Sex is mystical, much more than the movement of bodies — an act of worship to something he does not understand. It affirms his attractiveness, his youth, the fact that he is alive. He makes love with strangers like a child unturning stones in search of buried treasure; one there must be who will raise him to the ecstasy that he has glimpsed but never known. His search is erratic and, depending on mood, he is undiscriminating or eclectic, at times willing to be the other's fantasy, at times insistent on his own. Tonight he demands nothing, wants only to give, to award himself as the prize to whoever claims him.

David has eaten quickly, washed carelessly and now stands at the mirror combing his hair into place. He examines his face like a farmer inspecting a horse he wishes to buy. The skin has become thick, the lines long and deep. The eyebrows are heavy and the lips pursed into a permanent frown. Robin once told him that his meanness was attractive, that it was the maturity and strength of the heroes in Italian westerns.

Pushing money into a pocket, he goes slowly downstairs, mentally checking each room as he passes. At the front door he pauses and looks back at the gloomy hall and stairway leading up into darkness. He remembers with anger the disdainful expressions of many he has brought here. Then he pulls the door to, locks it and gets into the old car that sits by the gate.

Jack switches channels in search of some programme to hold his attention.

Another drink. Michael watches two or three faces, offers half-smiles more from habit than enthusiasm.

Although David prefers the anonymity and directness of those met in public conveniences, tonight he drives into the centre of town, only half-aware of the traffic around him.

The laughter of a comedy fades into the memory of the first day Jack knew he loved Michael. They were here, watching television, Jack in the armchair and Michael lying on the sofa, feet on its arm, head propped up on a cushion. He turned to make a comment about the newsreader and the angle of his head, the relaxation in his body and the friendly humour of his voice were the combination that opened Jack's mind. I love you, he said silently, unsure whether the emotion was overlaid by exuberance or despair.

The alcohol awakens memories of those Michael has loved, passions that have ended abruptly or in anger. The men he has wanted have been older, successful, their presence challenging him in ways he has not understood, although few have seen him as more than the casual partners that he himself has picked up. But emotions quickly roused have quickly died and he is an optimist, one who sees the past as only rehearsal for the future, who sees no difference between expectation and hope.

This bar David enters is never empty. He used to come here with Robin, who said it was the place to meet the most interesting people. David would sit in a corner fingering his glass, envious of Robin and jealous of the strangers with whom he laughed and chatted. Robin would look towards him, try and cajole him into a smile, then shrug and turn back to his companions' laughter. At home he loved Robin with an intensity that blotted out all other sensation; here he was struck numb by hostility and hate. But he has met other young men here, and he will do so again.

The news. Jack's thoughts rebound between Michael and the screen as if his mind were being plunged between scalding and freezing baths.

The only one watching Michael tonight is a stocky, dark-haired man in his forties whose intense appearance suggests long stories of a difficult childhood, a failed marriage and clumsy fumbling in bed. One more drink and he will decide whether to go home or try elsewhere.

The boy reminds David of Robin. He is shorter and darker, but has the same narrow face, moving eyes and, for others, ready smile. He has even glanced in David's direction, acknowledged the interest, then turned away.

Bored with television, Jack goes through to the kitchen and starts to clear up. The half-pie and vegetables for Michael are wrapped and placed in the refrigerator. Probably he will return having already eaten, and the next day ignore the left-overs in favour of some microwave meal. Uncertain whether his sudden anger is with Michael or himself, he tears off the cellophane and sweeps the food into the rubbish-bin.

Michael is aware of the first pangs of hunger. Jack will have prepared some food, will, in the off-handed manner that does not disguise his longing, offer it to him when he returns. Here in the pub there is only one steady stare, which intrigues but does not excite him. In a sudden gesture of impatience he drains the glass and leaves.

So soon? But he is the one David wants. Pushing between men standing alone and animated conversations, he walks out into the street. The figure he seeks is rapidly walking away, an image of arrogant youth in black jacket and trousers. David runs after him.

Jack's annoyance and energy takes him to the living-room, to his bedroom, where he straightens books, empties ashtrays and puts away clothes.

If Michael went home to Jack, it would be to admit defeat, to offer him hope where none exists. It is dark but not yet late, the streets are busy and there is still time for another bar, another crowd.

A gentle tap on the shoulder and "Hi"; the smile is always difficult.
    "Uh?" They all share the same scowl of curiosity and anger.
    "You just left the bar, didn't you?"
    "Yes."
    "I wanted to talk to you." The critical moment; if he hesitates, David has won.
    "Why didn't you?"
    "I am now. Where are you going?"
    "To another bar."
    "Why not come back to my place for a drink?"

There is little for Jack to do, for he is by nature tidy, and he soon finds himself back in the armchair staring at the blank screen.

This would never be Michael's first choice. This stranger is an odd character whose friendly words are at odds with his fierce expression, an older man than he is usually attracted to, in the dull clothes of someone who has never gone far in life. But drink has made him generous and there is nevertheless an air of competence about the man, a suggestion that sex will be more efficient and rewarding than the awkwardness Michael first credited him with.

Of course David knows that this is not Robin. This one is suspicious, but young enough to be interested. It is important to talk, but not too much, to make jokes and laugh a little. To play such a role is difficult, causes him to sweat and almost tremble with effort. But when the time comes, this boy, like all the others, will be happy to lie on David's bed and be made love to.

As if at the office, confronted by conflicting priorities that only he can resolve, Jack tries to distance himself from his emotions. He loves Michael and Michael does not love him. He is getting old, Michael is still young. Michael needs love but will not admit it. And so on and so on, the apparently cold analysis giving the impression of progress, of decisions being made and the situation being resolved.

A part of the city Michael does not know. Dilapidated terraced houses. They stop outside a garden littered with rubbish and a front door needing paint. The hall is dark and dirty and smells unclean. Involuntarily he compares this man with Jack and the house with their flat. He wants to leave but inertia and politeness make him stay.

Through the darkness David can see the boy's disapproval and disappointment. "I've only just moved in, haven't had time to clean up." He switches on the light in the kitchen. Two of the cats approach cautiously; the boy bends to stroke them, asks their names.

"What do you want to drink?"

"What've you got?"

"Most things." A cupboard opens to a dozen or so bottles.

"Whisky, please."

The boy sits on a chair, eyes wandering from unwashed dishes to cat bowls and the door into the back garden. Perhaps he is like Robin, for his presence and eyes suggest life and sex. As he hands the boy a glass, he feels the first tightening of desire and quickening of breath.

"What's your name?"

"Michael. What's yours?"

"David."

"Have you got a phone?"

"Sorry?"

"Have you got a phone? I always call my flatmate if I'm going to be home late."

A warning. "Is he your lover?"

A smile. "No, but he worries about me."

"Why?"

"It's a long story. Anyway, can I use the phone?"

"I don't have one. And," pre-empting, "there isn't a call-box near."

"It doesn't matter. But I can't stay long."

Common sense tells Jack, as it has told him for months, that Michael will never be his lover. But rationalisation speaks louder, convinces him that Michael will change his mind, and if not, that his love is so great that it can tolerate anything Michael does. But the greater his love, the greater the pain and the situation has become a whirlpool from which he cannot get free.

Through the drink the house depresses Michael; it is the home of someone who will never succeed. And Michael dislikes failure, does not even find it interesting. But sex is sex and he stumbles up the narrow stairs, following his host to the front bedroom. Here too there is the odour of dirt. Clothes lie on chairs and hang out of open drawers; shoes, books and newspapers litter the floor; a cat has come in and curled up in front of the gas fire. The bed is old and high and made of iron. With a stiffening in his groin that is more mechanical than desire, he starts to undress.

A whiter skin than David had imagined, and a fuller body. He watches the boy strip, pull off shirt and vest and look for somewhere to set them down. He waits for David to undo his own clothes, then removes his trousers and lies down on the bed. David switches off the light, leaving only the orange glow of the fire and the darker street-light muffled by curtains.

It is too early for bed, but Jack can read a book there. He must not wait for Michael if there is nothing to wait for. He switches off lights, checks the front door. The brightness in the bathroom is depressing.

At least the sheets are clean. Michael lies back, then reaches out dutifully as the older man stretches out on top of him. He kisses, holds and strokes the aging skin, but soon lies back, knowing that little more is expected.

David knows that this is not Robin. Robin, for all his faults, was passionate. Robin gave. To the very end Robin fought. This one is passive, wants to be dominated. They are all the same, warm bodies with hard pricks, not caring who they are with, not caring what they are doing. Once again anger surges out of lust.

Without realising it, Jack's mind has strayed from the book as his hand has strayed to his groin. He strokes himself, and though he tries to create other images, it is Michael's smiling eyes he sees, Michael's warm mouth he kisses, Michael's smooth and pale skin that he touches.

Eyes closed, made tired by the warmth of drink and fire, Michael can imagine anything. Stretching like a cat, feeling lips on his chest and a hand between his legs, he recalls other men and bedrooms, muscles, tanned bodies, urgent desires that mirrored his own. In the back of his mind he prepares once again to enter paradise.

As he kisses it, lets his hands wander its length and explore its crevices, David examines the body under him. It is thin, rough, at once unique and the sum of all the bodies that have lain here before and moaned and quivered at his bidding.

Jack moans.

Michael moans.

David reaches swiftly down for the rope that quickly binds one of Michael's hands then the other. They never guess and they never understand.

Jack wipes himself and drops the tissues to the floor.

Michael shouts and struggles, kicks out sharply until his legs are held and tied. The shout becomes a brief scream until a cloth is pushed into his mouth. Through his anger and terror he sees the man's face appear, tries to understand the expression of concern and pleasure.

David must catch his breath, looks down at the boy, sees the fear in his eyes, the rapid rise and fall of his chest, the limpness in his groin. He rests a hand upon the heart and feels its rapid beat.

For once Jack is not saddened by the solitary orgasm. He feels older and wiser, knows that Michael can and will love him, that he must only be patient.

Before switching off the light, he glances at the clock. Michael will be home soon or at least he will call.

Michael's body, at first tense, relaxes slowly as the man neither threatens nor strikes, but makes slow and careful love. His eyes closed again, as if the darkness can convince him that this is no more than a bad dream, he feels the tongue and lips on his body, reawakening his desire. He is as frightened by his own arousal as by the ropes that have burnt skin from his ankles and wrists. Half-choking on the rag in his mouth and the panting he cannot control, he raises his head and sees the man's eyes look up from where he holds Michael's erection in his mouth. The glance is cold, alive and passionless. The hands move up, caress Michael's chest and play with his nipples. Then they reach towards his throat and squeeze.

He bucks and heaves and turns his head and tenses and jerks every muscle in his body in the desperate effort to throw the man off. For a moment he succeeds, but there is a sharp pain across the side of his face, and as he recovers he realises that the fingers are there again, pulling slowly tighter and the pressure spreading outwards from his chest becomes desire in his groin and agony in his throat and the two sensations are the same and the dark, dark pressure grows and explodes.

David's orgasm comes later, in that magic hour when, released from its bonds, the body is still warm and flexible, his to do with whatever he wishes. Then he will wash and go downstairs, only returning the next morning to clear up as he has to clear up when one of the cats has been sick. There is no fear or remorse as there was after Robin and the first few that followed him. Nor is there regret, for there will always be others to take each boy's place.

Jack sleeps lightly, waiting for the telephone to ring.

A ROOM
TO LET

He was late and very apologetic. I had been more resigned than annoyed — it would not have been the first time that an appointment casually made had been casually forgotten. However, when he explained that first the tube had been held up and then he had been misdirected, I sympathised and let my expression of doubt melt into one of polite welcome. We went upstairs and I showed him the room. He was polite about it, criticised neither the dark wallpaper nor the overbearing wardrobe, asked only where the bathroom was and whether visitors were welcome. I repeated the terms and, as we made our way back down, suggested that he stay for a cup of tea.

He was on the point of refusing. I had noticed that once he had made his apology and taken stock of the situation he had decided it was not for him. It was hardly surprising, for I was more than twice his age. Even if I had not made the pass he expected, he would still see all fifty-year-olds living alone as essentially dull — fastidious queens or staid bachelors.

But it was cold outside, he had come a long way and I had not rested an arm on his shoulder or brushed my hand against his jeans. Besides, it was only polite and if he should after all consider moving in, it was as well to get to know the landlord beforehand. So I left him in the living-room while I put on a kettle in the kitchen and emptied a packet of biscuits onto a plate. As I waited for the water to boil I stared out of the window at the bare trees bowing in the wind. It was a dreary day in March, a time when I stay indoors too much, reading and listening to the radio; his presence, his Northern speech and mannerisms, made a welcome break. He was almost attractive, although his youth held a greater appeal than his looks. With his dark unkempt hair and restless eyes, he reminded me less of someone I had known than of someone I would have liked to have known years before.

"D'you paint?" he asked when I came in.

"Not now. Those" — two or three unframed portraits over the fireplace — "are ten, fifteen, years old."

"They're good."

"Thank you." He meant he liked them. They lacked subtlety and were no more than competent.

"It's a nice room, this."

"I like it." I had made it bright and uncluttered, with furniture that was neither heavily nostalgic nor uncomfortably modern.

"So you want to live in London," I went on, when we had settled and had cups in our hands.

"Yeah."

"Why? To look for work?" If so, I imagined a long search and disappointment; he suggested no skill, no eagerness that Londoners of similar age lacked.

"No. Well, I mean yes, but I'm not expecting it to be easy."

"Then why?"

"It's somewhere new, different." He sat stiffly in his chair, less nervous than unsure of the situation. I wondered if he was naturally polite or still of an age that saw every elder as authority.

"Could you get a job?"

He shrugged. "I were a mechanic at home. I've got me certificate. I might be lucky."

"Car mechanic?"

He nodded. "What do you do?"

"Nothing." He looked blank. "I retired early," I went on. "I used to work in insurance."

"What do you do all day?"

"Read, go to museums. Swim. I still draw from time to time."

"Sounds boring to me.

"Why do you want a lodger?" he suddenly asked.

"The room's empty. I could do with the extra income." It was only partly a lie.

He leaned forward for a biscuit, sat back more relaxed, used to the idea that I was not trying to angle him into bed. There was certainly a sexuality about him, exaggerated rather than muffled by the careless way he dressed, but it was years since I had been attracted by youth or good looks alone.

"Have you seen many rooms?" I asked.

"Five. No, six."

"No good?"

"Two were all right, not the others. But they didn't want me."

"Why not?"

"Dunno. Perhaps they thought I wouldn't be able to pay."

"Have you looked for work?"

"Not much point, is there? Till I've got somewhere to stay. And that's not easy. One of the places I went to, they said I was the tenth person to ring up in two days. Right dump it were too. And prices are twice what they are up North." His eyes were fierce with indignation.

"You're the sixth person to look at that room."

"None of the others wanted it?"

"Two did, but I didn't want them."

"No?"

"The first went on about music and painting as if he'd slept with Britten and Hockney. The second made a pass at me."

His eyebrows rose. I tried not to smile. "Didn't you fancy him?"

"No. He saw me as a father-figure. That's the last thing I am."

"What are you then?"

The question surprised me and I began not merely to tolerate but to like him. "I don't have a role, if that's what you mean. I'm just a middle-aged man who's not quite in tune."

"What do you mean?"

I warned myself to think more carefully before I spoke. "Nothing really. It's a false pride to think we're somehow different or special."

There was a pause in which I poured us both more tea. The wind had got up again and was throwing rain against the window. The room had darkened and I switched on a table-lamp. It made him look older, more tired and worn, as if he were on drugs or had not slept for nights. I was not repelled but more attracted by this suggestion of a character that I was beginning to discover. I looked at myself from his point of view and wondered whether he saw an individual or merely another grey-haired old man with the expression of amused contentment that always annoys the young.

"Have you been to London before?" I asked.

"Twice. Once when I were thirteen with me parents, and again last year."

"Like it?"

"It's all right."

"It must be, if you're coming to stay here."

He looked uncomfortable.

"Are you coming to London or running away from home?"

"I'm not running away." His indignation returned. "Everyone knows where I am."

"That isn't what I meant."

He subsided. "A bit of both, I suppose."

"I don't see you as the type to run to a place. I'd think you'd be quite happy at home."

He let that sink in. "Maybe. But things were getting on top of me, so I thought I'd come and have a look here. Make a change."

"Things?"

He wondered whether to go on. "I had this affair. We were really good mates. We'd known each other since I left school."

"Your age?"

"He's a couple of years older, but it didn't matter. It were like we were the same age."

I waited. Now that he had started he would go on.

"I didn't know he were gay at first, and he didn't know about me. We met each other one night in the local cottage. I'd just gone in there on me way home, 'cause I'd been drinking, but he used it regularly. I got quite a shock, 'cause I'd always fancied him and there he was." He grinned at the memory.

"Why did you fancy him?"

He thought about it. "He's. . . he's friendly and kind. And he's really good-looking. I don't know. I can't explain it. I just feel good when I'm with him."

"What happened?" I prompted as the story seemed to drift away.

"We couldn't have sex that night, because we were both still living at home and I wouldn't do it in public. We talked about it, though, and decided to get a place of our own. Me mam couldn't understand it. She thought I were daft, but me dad thought it were a good idea — looking after meself."

"And?"

"It were all right at first; we got on really well. But then I discovered he'd been going back to the cottage. He prefers that to having sex with me."

Each to their taste. I thought of the risks, of the smell of public conveniences, of figures looking round furtively as their hands clasped their groins. I could not see this youth before me there.

"It weren't just the sex," he went on. "It were something more. I thought it were to him too, but I was wrong. He prefers rougher types. He just wants us to be friends."

I looked across, saw the thinly disguised pain. It was a relief to be older, to be past the stage of doubts and worries, to know that the ultimate satisfaction was in being alone.

"So you've left him."

"I suppose so. But I've got to go back and get me things. What's so funny?" he asked sharply as I let myself smile.

"What you mean is, you're giving him another chance."

"No, I'm not."

"Well, why didn't you bring everything with you, if you really wanted a break?"

"I might decide to stay up North, just move into me own place." His defiance was only momentary. "I suppose you're right," he went on. "But it's. . . I love him."

"Do you?"

"What do you know about it?" his voice filled the room.

"You've not known me half an hour and you've not met Len at all. There're so many things about him; I really love him. Haven't you ever been in love?"

"I don't know," I said. "I've lived with someone. Two people, in fact, one for five years and the other for ten."

"Oh." So perhaps I did know what I was talking about. "What happened?"

"Arthur — the first one — was killed in a car crash. Tom left me."

He let a moment pass. "Weren't you cut up by that? Tom, I mean."

"No. I was relieved. I'd begun to realise that you don't need other people. Or I don't. Arthur was different. If he was alive, I think we'd still be together." And though Arthur had died nearly twenty years before, his laughter and enthusiasms were sharper in my memory than the greyness of Tom.

"Isn't that love?"

"I prefer to call it respect."

The question went through his mind as to whether he respected Len. He was no fool, no more than others of his age. I realised that I was enjoying talking to him, yet at the same time I was aware that at any moment my patience might break and I would wish him out onto the street. He was, after all, only another confused young man, no different in essence from the rest, convinced that his pain was not only harsh but unique. If he were to stay I would see myself burdened with his problems and emotions, becoming alternately a shoulder to cry on and a doll to stick pins in. I wondered again what had possessed me to consider letting the room.

"I don't think. . ." he began.

"What?"

"Nothing. I was going to say."

"You were going to say that you love someone and I've never really loved, so I've no right to talk about it."

"Something like that."

"I've been through it. Love is a disease of youth; most of us go through it. A few are cured, the rest are disabled." Again I regretted the triteness of words spoken without thought.

"I suppose you've been 'cured'. But I don't want to be."

"Don't you?"

For a moment there was doubt in his eyes, then it was rejected. "You're very cynical."

"I'm not in the least cynical. I'm realistic. I've had experience."

"But I love Len. I think about him, I worry about him, I want to be with him, make love with him, all the time."

"You're infatuated by him. You're seeing what you want to see, not what he really is." I wondered if I had gone too far, but he did not react. "Does he love you?"

"Not in the same way." It was obviously a question he had asked himself before; the honest answer was no.

"Do you think he ever will?"

"I don't know." Again no. I did not feel sorry for him. It was all experience with a capital E, the process of Growing Up. If for him it was more painful, that only proved his naivety, his eagerness to trust.

"How long did you live together?" I asked, reluctant now that the subject had been brought up to leave it only half-discussed.

"Six months."

"Does he know why you're in London?"

"More or less."

"What did he say?"

"About why I'm here? Not much. He said it were my life to do as I wanted."

"And what do you want?"

"I don't know."

Suddenly the whole conversation was futile. There was no point in telling him that he was not worried about losing Len but about losing the idea of love, losing the security he thought he had found. He could only work that out for himself. I was no *deus ex machina* whose intervention would set him on a less troublesome path. Nor could I be sure that what little I had said, the hints I had given him, would take seed, for in the days and weeks to come he would be influenced by other words more often repeated and more willingly listened to.

Yet I was reluctant to let him go, to return to my solitude. Young he might be, but he was less arrogant than most. He was even willing to reflect, if not always concede. I might not wish him as a lodger but I was happy to let him stay as the afternoon drifted on into evening, to listen to him talk and watch him react. "More tea?" I offered. "I can boil the kettle again."

"I should be going."

"That's up to you."

"Then yes, please."

He followed me into the kitchen, asking questions about the housework as if suddenly remembering his original intention for coming here. I told him I expected no more than that care be taken not to spill things and that dishes be washed by the end of the day. Looking over my small collection of condiments, he surprised me by saying that he liked to cook; it was an activity that for me had never been enjoyable.

When we sat down again the mood had changed, the confessional had yielded to the conversational. He talked about cars, in particular a model that had been built years ago and which he wanted to buy if he ever had the money. He spoke with such enthusiasm and knowledge that it would have been more true to say he had a love affair with motor vehicles than with any empty-headed youth in whichever town he came from. I found myself listening fascinated to a subject I knew little about and if he had asked me at that moment to go out to inspect and dirty my hands on the workings of some engine, I would happily have done so, even under the rain.

At last, however, the teapot emptied, the subject died and he said he had to go. As he stood up, his awkwardness returned and I found myself faced once again with the shy and unappealing youth who had appeared at my door.

"You know your way back to the tube station?" I asked as we looked out at the street where the wind still blew but the rain was weakening.

He nodded. "Thanks for the tea. What do I do if I want the room?"

It had almost slipped my mind. "That's up to you. Ring if you want it."

"That might not be until next week."

"That doesn't matter. I doubt that it'll have gone."

"Okay." He seemed reluctant to leave.

"Think over what I said about Len."

"Mm." Half-protesting, he walked out. "I will." At the gate he turned to speak.

"What was that?"

"I said I think I'd like living here."

"Oh." I half-smiled. "Goodbye."

I went in, closed the door and cleared up in the living-room. He never rang back, thank Heaven.

DISCOTHEQUE — FOUR VOICES

Tube noisy, shaky, empty. Old woman beside me, Rasta over there, headphones on, deaf and blind to the world. In the black window opposite I can almost see me. Hair good, eyes not clear, no, everything is good. I stood in front of mirror and saw strength and arrogance of make-up, clothes and eye. Jacket new, white, training pants white with blue streaks, suggesting energy, sex, life. White is good, shiny white is pure, sexy. Blue is light, blue is life.

Train stops, doors open, yellow light, couple get in. One more stop. I want to be there, to strip off, to dance. I am different, I am me, I can dance, I will dance, I am dance. Others pretend, others play, others sleep, others die, die, die. I live, I do, I dance. My body moves, my body lives, it is long, strong. I live, I dance.

Train stops. Get out. Along platform, up escalator. Others around me, going too. Couples kissing, holding, couples. I am alone. No John. I am now alone. No John. I will always be alone. Punk, denim, no style. I have style. I have style and colour and life and dance. I walk on air. I'm walking on air through dark street. No one can touch me, no one can see me. Everyone can see me, everyone can envy me. I have strength, smoothness, power, attraction, life. I can fly.

Always a queue. Fat, ugly doormen. Bored girl taking money. On and in, on and in. Here, against the wall, by the cloakroom, stop and strip, peel off clothes, watch those watching me, wanting me. They want me, want my body, want my life. Fold jacket, fold pants, put in bag. Hand bag over. I am naked, I am free. I am savage, I am warrior. I come to dance, stomp, circle, burn, celebrate, destroy. I am war-chief, I am king.

On, on. Door opens, light, music, life explodes. I leap up, touch ceiling, stretch out arms and legs and land. I am alive. I twist, I turn. Around me people stand and talk and drink and walk and look at each other and they're dull and drab and dreary. Not everybody. That gold cape, gold hair, gold face. He is trying, but he has buried himself. He does not have style, he does not have life. That girl does, however, that girl who laughs and looks at me. And there is John, with his back to me, same jeans, same stance, same thick curly hair. Then he turns and I see and I know and I remember that John is dead, that John will always be dead.

It is a vast cavern, another world. The gods shine down on us, play for us, call to us. This is eternity, I can stay here forever. I can dance and dance and learn to fly. Here, where we move and live and laugh and cry, is where I belong. We are the warriors come to celebrate, to dance the dance of life, the dance of death. I am the chief come to sacrifice, the virgin come to die.

They watch, they always watch. They watch my body with its muscles, so clear, so hard, they stare at my briefs, they want my cock, they stare at my legs. John loved my legs. They watch me dance, watch me move, some mock but they all admire. I have the courage to be myself, to be free, to live. So they move apart, let me pass, and I come onto the floor and the lights flash and the music surrounds me and my body begins to move. Legs up, down, left, right, arms out, curve, straight, body hunch, round, straighten, arms, legs, armslegsarmsbodyoutleftthumpthump-thump green red green red white green dark green dark green dark red thump thump thump voice "I'll always be there" thump thump snake across snake of light snake of sound thump thump round up back hot thump thump sweat thump thump waterfall of sound thunder of light up up "for you for you for you" thump thump faces arms legs denim black dress stare thump thump thump and on and on and on

I walk slowly, carefully, a model on a catwalk, a cat on a tightrope, along corridors, up stairs, round a balcony and back down to the main floor. My eyes are never still, creep like a prowling thief from one person to the next, from face to body to crotch to face. They are my guides and my censors, yet when they approve I do not stop to appraise but walk on, nervous and afraid, seldom turning back to wonder and hope. My courage is truly dutch – I need alcohol to cruise as a weightlifter needs his steroids – and the drink I have poured has not yet had time to pore. So I go to the bar and full glass in hand stand at the edge of the dance floor looking out to sea and trying to focus on the waves.

A silhouette here, movement there, a bright shirt in the darkness signals and vanishes. I strain into the night and catch only bobbing hair and flickering faces; out of the whirlpool an arm, a body, an expression appears and is dragged down. I focus on a smile and it has soured into a scowl, watch a T-shirt sag as its strength dissolves, a man vanish where he should stand forever. Am I growing old or was I never able to see clearly through lights that flash from brilliance to darkness, from point to flood, from one colour to the next, bursts of magic that transform age into youth, beauties into beasts, flesh into fantasy and my despair into desire? It is all as vague as a dream, as vague as the dream lover who I search and long for. All I can be sure of is those who are near me, those whose reality cannot be denied.

Two men in dresses with painted faces and blinding blond hair clomp energetically. A tall thin individual's moustache is as serious and heavy as the movements he makes. A dark-haired youth in sleeveless shirt pirouettes, bounces, leaps and dives, laughing, grinning, watching his partner. His body is slim, tight, young, he moves with such energy, he is so happy, he would make me laugh, he would bring my tea in bed, would make things and paint things; I want him, I want him, I want him, but he sees only his partner, his lover, his accomplice, a dull man in black who rocks unimaginatively from side to side, watching with the pride and self-satisfaction of possession. If I stood, if I stayed, if I stared, if I stabbed between them with my eyes, letting the ache in my chest, in my mouth, in my groin, pour out, I could not prise them apart, would never see that youth, that wondrous youth, dance for me.

Away. Another round. A policeman on his beat, watching the crowds, the passers-by, the suspicious loiterers, ready to pull one or more in for questioning. I begin to recognise them, to know who I have rejected and who I wish to inspect again. Yet as I walk past I feel and fear their returning stares. Everything is too open, too honest, too searching, too abrupt. I need a one-way mirror so I can watch and choose at my leisure, examine their stance and expression, practise my lines and smile. Then when ready, rehearsed, I could swoop and sweep them away. Instead, all they see and hear is my hesitation, my concentration, my verbation . . .

Open shirt and jeans, ankle boots and ruffled hair. He offers strength and reassurance, quiet drinks in country pubs, pleasant home, a recent car. My courage well and truly screwed, I go and talk and am rewarded by monotonous monosyllables and perfunctory politeness. Yes, no, sometimes, no thank you. A bore, a stuck-up insufferable bore. Sour grapes, sour grapes; you're too old to be angered or hurt by rejection. Move on, move on.

Back at the dance floor the rhythm is faster, the lights brighter. Two hundred, three hundred people together. I look from one to the next like a bee at the end of summer hunting for pollen. One is too old, another's too short, too fat, too feminine, too unfriendly, has the wrong fetish, wrong sex, wrong clothes or expression. The ones I want, the one I want, lurks beyond like a chameleon behind his brethren. A blond in blue shirt and black trousers, a crewcut stripped and sweating to the waist, curly hair and warm eyes in incongruous pullover. They shift in and out of my vision, tumbling arms, swinging hips, turning legs, as if I were invisible, as if I did not exist.

My gaze bounces from floor to ceiling, my eyes blur and refocus, searching through the forest of cotton and denim. There a mirage, shimmering in the stormy light, white briefs tight over pumping buttocks, framed by bare back and bare legs. He turns, blue and white make-up streak from his eyes, dance across his chest, dive into his groin. He is not handsome, but his nose and jaw are strong and sweat drips down his cheeks from his damp and dark hair. He has no expression, is as unseeing as if hypnotised or drugged or mindless. His chest is strong and the sweat flows down, down, over the hollow of his stomach to be absorbed by the band of white. There his sex is veiled, virginal, vigilant. He has the legs of a runner and when he turns I can see the ripple of his backbone, the dancing shoulderblades and lean hollows of his hips. I want to take him, to have and to hold him, to kiss and lick and stroke and arouse. He would be mine to make as I wish and yet he would never change. He would listen and learn and yet be my teacher. He would lie in my bed, our bed, and be made love to, he would overpower me and make me his. We would fight and forgive, leave and live and love each other. He is everything I desire, he is my desire and he is here before me, he is here for me.

Coming down is not natural, coming down is pain, coming down is returning to life after the oblivion of death. I want to dance for ever, I want to live for ever, I want to forget for ever. John and I danced, John and I danced, when he was tall and strong and loved me and we danced here and made love here and my hips ground into his and I felt his cock, I felt his love and we danced here when he was old and thin and tired and I watched him and could not cry and watched him and could not cry.

Coming down is forced by tiredness and thirst, slipping from the groove. Don't want to leave, but slip, through, out, up to bar. Wait, order drink, wait, turn. They pretend not to watch, but they do, they do. They want my mouth and my nipples and my stomach and my cock, they want to kiss my legs, to run their hands up, to feel the muscles, to feel the hair, to grasp, to stroke, they want to reach slowly up, to hear me gasp, to feel the ache, the desire, they want their mouth on my cock, I want John's mouth on my cock, they want to suck, to suck my life from me.

I won't, I can't, I won't, I can't. I am John's, I can only be John's. I will not be theirs, I cannot be theirs. If only there were another John, but there isn't another John, there will never be another John.

Someone talks, I turn. Tall, dark, balding, putting on weight, trying to impress, wanting to reach out, put his hand on my body, John's body. He talks and talks. The same words, always the same words. He has nothing, he is nothing. Finish drink, smile. Back to dance floor. Wait, look round, perhaps someone . . . No, never, dance, dance, dance.

If the figures aren't on my desk by lunchtime, she will have to go. I don't care what personal problems she has, they can't interfere in business. I shouldn't have taken her on in the first place, but these agencies are so bloody persistent. All they're interested in is their commission. "Mr Wright, we've found someone who's ideal for you. She's been two years with Securicor and is looking for a more responsible position." Or whatever they said. They all sound as wonderful as their own adverts. And I was taken in. She was very smart, very competent at the interview. There was no reason not to hire her. And then I discover she's paranoid, neurotic, incapable, loses files, forgets appointments, thinks the other girls are down on her, calls in sick every other week, and I have to put in time doing my own secretary's job.

Another drink. It's always the third one that brings me down to earth, that makes the office seem less important, that convinces me for a time that it does not matter that we have been making a loss for over a year, that it is my job to cut expenditure, to tell Derek and Roger we cannot afford this or that. It's not Roger that's the problem, it's Derek. He hates my guts, he's looking for an excuse to get rid of me. I have to be careful, because if I lose this job, God knows where I'll find another. No one wants a middle-aged rat from a sinking ship.

Well, perhaps today it's the fourth drink that'll remind me it's half-past midnight and I'm in a discotheque and what I need is a really good fuck. There are some quite attractive faces and bodies around if I can remember to look at them, maybe even smile and talk and I'll forget about the office and Andrew at home.

Andrew at home. Or Andrew at a disco, this disco, maybe I'll see him here. No, I won't. It would be beneath him. This is the kind of place he'd go to a few times at university, as he'd smoke pot and sleep with one or two women to see what it's like and be patronising about it for the rest of his life. God, he's become intolerant. No, that's not true. He's always been intolerant; I just used to admire it, think it was strength of character. A strong personality, a sense of humour and loving nature, that's what I bought a house with. And what have I got now but an intolerant cynic who suspects me of screwing with every man who looks at me twice. Who'll either be awake when I get in or who'll make bitchy comments first thing in the morning. And he thinks it's adolescent to go to discos!

I just need to get laid. Have another drink. Forget work, forget Andrew, forget everything and find a man. Five drinks since I came in. I have to stop.

How long has he been beside me? I expect people to be outrageously dressed in here, but not like that. Look at the sweat dripping down him, look at those muscles, look at that basket. He's practically naked; all I need do is hook my finger in there and pull down and . . . He must be available. He wouldn't be dressed like that, undressed like that, otherwise. He wants to be picked up, he wants to be taken home and fucked. And I want to be the one to do it, even if it costs me, fifty, a hundred. He won't refuse. He needs it; whether it's the sex or money, he needs it.

You must be hot. Been dancing a lot. I like the colours; does the design mean anything? I thought maybe it was something to do with Red Indians. It's not very busy tonight. I haven't seen you here before. It's been a long day for me, how about you? Like a drink? Where do you live? Are you doing anything later? Maybe I can give you a ride home.

He may walk away, he may think he's turned me down, that I'll take the hint, that I'll go and find some pretty little teenager who'll be glad of an extra thirty or forty quid. But I don't want a doll. I want a man. I want him and I'm going to get him. He's gone to the dance floor. I'll follow and stand and watch and stare at him, until he gets used to the idea. Because that's what he wants, that's why he's dressed like that, even if he doesn't know it. It's an open invitation to anyone and I'm going to make sure I'm the one to get it.

There he is in the centre. Easily visible, despite the irritating flashing lights and all the others around him. No one else seems to notice him. Not true; I can see one or two with their eyes on him. He dances well, with the music, with variety. That body can move, the hips grind, pump, thrust. I want to take him, like that, sweaty, tired, out of breath, not quite sure where he is, throw him over my desk, rip off his pants and fuck him in the middle of the reports and the unanswered letters and the forward accounts, fuck him so that he shouts and brings that stupid woman in to shriek and throw up her hands in horror, fuck him so that the whole room shakes, the oh-so-decorative plants by the window fall off their stand and crash through the glass, fuck him as if he were Derek or Andrew screaming for mercy, fuck him so hard that the whole building collapses around us, fuck him so hard that nothing in the world is left except him and me.

My head expands, my body glows. I am the king, I am the warrior, I am the virgin. I am free, I am music, I am light, I am strong, I am sex, I am life, I am me. I move, I am naked, I am God, God moves, I move, my armslegsbody move, I am cock, I am ass, I am cock, hard, thrusting, I am ass, open, welcoming, I am all they desire, I am movement, I am energy, I am light. I dance, I fuck, I dance, I am fucked. With John I fucked, he loved my body, I loved his body, before, before, before. He was strong, he was handsome, not thin, not thin and old. I don't want to remember, I don't want to remember. Move, move, move, up, down, round, free, I am free, I am free.

I am two minds, one dances, the other watches. One is free, one is laughing. They see and pretend not to see. They want and pretend not to want. They want to fuck, I want to fuck, but not with them, not with them. My prick and ass are my heart, my soul, my all. They want but they cannot have. The white cloth, the chastity, the purity protects, protects and reveals. What they want and cannot have. I am vulnerable and I am free.

They approach, hungry eyes, desperate eyes, dance around me, dance at me, want me want me want me but I am not here, I do not want, I am, I dance, I dance. He dances too, tries to hold me with his eyes, happy eyes, and shirt and jeans. He is a mirror, his eyes follow mine, his legs follow mine, his arms follow mine. He wants me. Yes, maybe, perhaps, one day. One day in the future, a long time from now, you and I, you and I. But not today, not tonight; I am not here. I am in the music, the light, the dance. I am not here. I am free, I am strength, I am sweat, I am sex, I am free.

On and on and on and on. My life myself I exist this is me, this is me, this is me. Nothing before, nothing after. No John. No illness and death, no tears and pain, no love, no love, no love. I want, he is gone gone gone. I am alone I am now I am nothing nothing before nothing after. Black black black silent silent silent still still on on on

Sometimes those two go over a top. A joke's a joke but if it were a cow they'd milk its corpse. It's time I left them alone and went for a walk to see what was on offer tonight. I didn't come here to listen to their double act. I suppose I came to look around, see if there's anything interesting and if there was pick him up. Maybe just to talk, not even have sex! How time's have changed; I remember sitting on old Uncle Michael's knee, listening wide-eyed and open-mouthed to his tales of Islington Cottage. "There was one old queen who used to turn up every evening, take his false teeth out, slip them into his pocket and stuff a cushion under his knees. There'd be a queue out onto the pavement and always one local bobby on his way back to the nick. With his helmet off, of course, so no one would recognise him."

Stop it. You're getting as bad as the others. Well, what have we here? I thought the cowboy look died with Ronald Reagan's last coherent sentence. Or maybe he's up from some weird club in the East End. Doesn't he know it's the tramp look these days? Unshaven, long dirty coats and a look of dementia or debility. And that's just the women.

Stop it! Be serious. Look through this assembly of masculinity in all its variety and choose the one that's suitable for *you*. I mean, somewhere out there there must be someone six foot tall, twenty-three or thereabouts, with the mind of Einstein, the wit of Coward and the looks of Tom Cruise, whose one aim in life is to meet and fall passionately in love with the manager of a pet shop and the proud possessor of a Mini that's had more spent on it in repairs in the last month than it was ever worth when it was new. Not to mention the menagerie at home and the flatmate who insists on playing classical music at the volume of heavy metal.

Now that one's very attractive. Well, the body could do with a bit of an overall, but I like the face. Sort of cute and knowing. The kind of guy who'd send embarrass-the-boss telegrams and swear he had nothing to do with it. But he's with someone. Onto the next. And very quickly onto the one after that; why do some people assume that a leather jockstrap makes even the scraggiest body desirable? There should be a law against it. There probably is.

I watched that one earlier in the evening. It's not so much the face but the way he dresses — trendy enough to show he knows what he's doing, but not so trendy that he doesn't have a mind of his own. He even smiled. I should have gone over then. But now he's talking to someone, maybe he was with him all the time. It's too late, too late, all the best fruit has gone.

Well, who needs sex, anyway? Quarter of an hour on the dance floor is just as satisfying. More so, because you can do whatever you want. Not that I'm a great dancer. In fact I prefer dancing alone. There's nothing more embarrassing or stupid than to dance with someone for half an hour and not once look at him in the eye. You might as well dance alone. So, squeeze into the middle, try not to get hit by that drunken woman or that skinhead who looks as if he's had constipation for a week, find yourself a space and shake yourself about a bit.

Why is it the most attractive ones are always taken up? Okay, I know it's not true; I just need an excuse. I mean that boy in the white T-shirt. He probably works out three times a week, looks intelligent, moves like he's good in bed and is staring into his lover's eyes as if hypnotised. Turn round, look elsewhere. Oh, cheeky! Does he want us to think he's walked off the beach? And what's that he's got on his body and face? Okay, admit it, the colour's striking. So's he. And, it seems, alone. I'll bet you no one's had the courage to go up and talk to him. Beauty often puts people off. And he is, well, not beautiful. Hunky, gorgeous, sexy, built and, from the looks of it, hung. Who cares if his face won't launch a thousand ships. Look at those thighs, that chest, that etcetera.

Faint heart never won hunky youth. Get over there, dance with him. That's what he likes, that's what he understands. Go and strut your stuff, do your thing, stare him out, draw him on. No one else is. Let yourself go. Just dance. Don't stare at him, don't think about him, relax, let the music take over, be aware, that's all, be aware, feel your body sway, your arms surge, your legs pound and pound and turn and leap and lunge and see him, see his muscles, see them flex and stretch and curve, and he is dancing and I am dancing fast and my eyes are half-closed and his hips move from side to side and I move with him and his backside seems to grind into my groin and he turns and leans back and offers me his cock and I could reach out and take it but that would be going too far and I swing with him and there is only darkness with torchlight flashing from the ceiling and the music is fast, fast and I look at him and he seems to be smiling and his back is to me again, moving faster than I ever could and he turns and I look at him and we dance together and as I move in one direction he moves in the other, too fast for me, too flexible, too energetic and we move together and he moves apart and I turn and he is further away and I look at him and he doesn't see me and another body comes between us and the music has caught me and I can't stop, I dance and I dance and I dance and so does he but he is further away and there is someone between us and he does not care he never cared.

I dance alone. Maybe I expect too much. I should wait until he is tired, comes off for a rest, or wait until the end, talk to him then. I'll just stand at the edge of the floor, watching. He'll get tired, he'll come off sometime. And then we can talk or have a drink or do whatever he wants to do.

On and on and on. Light and music, light and music, red, green, white, blue, red, green blue white red black redblackred thump, thump, thump, layers of music like layers of earth, layers of a river flowing at different speeds, deep sounds, dark sounds, shallow sounds, light sounds, on into the sea, into oblivion, into death, round and round, reach and point, thump and thump, sense muscles, sense movement, sense sweat, thump, thump, from hair to toes, swirl, dive and surge, dive and surge. Others around, frozen water, frozen movement, camera caught, backs and shoulders, faces and hair, awkward, graceful, watching, ignoring, thump thump thump

Thirsty, want to drink, want to piss, can't stop, must dance, must move, must leap must dance must dance. What's the time where am I who am I what am I I I. I am river I am warrior I am light I am music I am movement. Body sex movement sex movement movement movement. Someone watching, always watching, good, good. Dance more, dance faster. Still there, always there, dancing with me, dancing around me. Jeans, red shirt, red belt red belt. Go away, stay, go away, go stay go stay go stay. Dancing with me I dance faster, fucking with me I fuck faster. He wants my body, my tits, my prick, my ass, he wants me. Fuck off fuck off fuck fuck fuck. So close I can touch him dance him fuck him. His face his face round, wanting, funny, bright, eyes, bright eyes. But but he isn't John, I can't reach him, I mustn't reach him, I don't want him, jeans, belt, shirt, red, dark blue, red, dark blue

I dance with John, only John, I fuck with John, only John. Strong John, kind John, thin John, dying John, dance, dance. John loved me, John loves me, John loves me, John here, John dying, John moving spinning shouting leaping laughing holding kissing stroking kissing fucking kissing falling kissing crying kissing ill kissing ill ill ill

He never stops. He dances on and on like a vision come to haunt me. His hair is matted, his body soaked, the make-up patchy and no one sees him except me and I stand on the sidelines like a spectator at a football match, like a boy on the shore, as if there

were a great gulf between us that I could never cross. And if I
spend all evening doing this he will never notice me, will walk off
when the music stops, stride past me as if I were no more than
a scattered chair, a fallen glass. If I want him I have to go after
him. I have to get in there, get in and place myself in front of him,
so that he sees me, he knows me and then and then

Two hundred pounds. Whatever he wants he can have, but I
must have him. I want that body. The world can go hang, Andrew
can throw a fit, the firm can collapse tomorrow, but I want that
body. I want to have it, to fuck it, to rape it, to have him begging
for more, to have him down on his knees, crying, pleading,
desperate. And I will pay; whatever it takes I will pay. But I have
to have him. I will go over there and stop him. No one ever got
what they wanted by waiting for the other chap to snap it up.

Still jiving. And I have to stand here catching my breath. You're
out of condition, old son. Remember the days when you could
knock back ten pints, knock off ten houses, knock up ten birds,
knock down ten cars and still run a four-minute mile? What you
need is a Bullworker. Or a bull. Or at least a stud. Or that stud.
He is definitely cute, would grace anybody's black satin sheets.
So get back in there, dance with him again. He's really desperate
for you, he's drooling over your overweight body. He's just shy;
these strong silent types usually are. Einsteins in Schwarzenegger
bodies never have any self-confidence. Go back, smile sweetly at
him, pick him up in your arms and walk, stagger, gracefully off
the floor.

Faster faster faster I am music I am light I am light I am
everything I am everywhere I am I am I am John my muscles live
my body lives I live I die I am I dance I am I I I I

My stomach feels like stone.

I could set him up. Give him a flat. The money'll come from
somewhere.

Come on boy, come to Daddy, come on home.

Wet hot blind flash thump thump thump thump

He's a god.

He's it.

He's ill.

John eyes John dies the music dies eyes giant's voice light light whirlwind dies room spins thump thump a face faces I live I die he smiles I smile he they I

He

    collapses

        to the floor.

TRAIN
OF
EVENTS

"A phantom faggot? On the tube?" Geoff laughed. "Now I've heard everything."

"I didn't say he was a phantom." Philip's patience was beginning to wear thin. "All I said was that he reminded me of the Flying Dutchman. He's always travelling and every time I try and get near him he always disappears."

"You mean he has a wild look in his eye, a hook for a hand and clogs on his feet?" Geoff looked round for others to share the joke.

"I hardly think so," I interrupted, conscious that Philip was about to lose his temper. That was sometimes the problem with bringing strangers together for Sunday lunch — good humour could not be guaranteed. Although I agreed with Geoff that the story sounded ridiculous, Philip, as my oldest friend, deserved my loyalty. "You try squeezing through a carriage in the rush hour to get to someone you recognise. You can hardly shout at him to wait."

"Of course not," said Sunil. "After all, we're all British, aren't we?"

That little irony was lost as Bill, a software writer, tried to analyse the problem in terms he could understand. "Let me get this straight. You say that almost every time you travel by underground you see the same guy?"

"That's right." Philip was obviously relieved to be taken seriously.

"What does he look like? Is he always dressed the same?"

"He's probably about six feet, thick fair hair, slim, very attractive. Of course he changes his clothes. Yesterday it was a leather jacket with faded jeans. Today it was one of these bulky canvas anoraks, two-tone. I don't remember the trousers. Oh, and the earring was different today. It used to be a black stud."

I stopped myself from commenting that the description resembled nearly every man Philip had lost his heart to in the five years that I had known him.

"He's unlikely to be a ghost if he doesn't wear the same clothes," Bill pronounced.

"Why?" asked Geoff. "Don't ghosts have wardrobes?"

"I suppose they could," Bill conceded, taking the question at face value. "And you see him every time you travel by tube?" he turned back to Philip.

"Every time I get in the gay carriage."

"The what?" Geoff asked, eyebrows exaggeratedly raised. I resolved not to invite him to lunch again. "What is a gay carriage? One that lusts over other carriages of the same sex?"

"No," said Philip, exasperated. "On every line there's a coach that gay people are supposed to travel on. On the Piccadilly it's the second. On the District it's the last; the Central Line it's either of the central carriages."

"Says who?"

"I don't know. I read it somewhere."

"Utter rubbish," Geoff commented.

"No more rubbish than walking around with coloured handkerchiefs sticking out of your back pocket," I said.

"That's different," he protested.

"Is it?" I asked, less interested in handkerchiefs than in preserving Philip's self-respect. I was in fact concerned. Ever since the brief period when we had been lovers Philip, now twenty-seven, had become less and less in touch with daily life.

Protected from poverty by a family inheritance, he drifted from job to job, individual to individual, making few friends and fewer relationships. Living nearby, I was the only person he saw regularly.

"*Anyway,*" Philip regained everyone's attention. "I keep seeing him. In the rush hour. In the evening when I go into town. On the last train going home. Sometimes there're only two or three of us in the carriage and he's sitting a few feet away. Recently he's started cruising me properly. So a couple of times I've gone up to speak to him and he hasn't been there." The last few words were almost a wail.

"It sounds like a figment of your imagination," Geoff's tone was just short of contempt. "When did you last get laid?"

That was too close to the bone. "What's your theory, Sunil?" I asked.

"I don't have one," he said. It bothered me that he looked bored. Of those around the table he was the one who I knew least and whose presence and ideas interested me most. If he saw these other friends as a reflection of my own personality, it would not be long before I lost him.

"Shall we change the subject?" I suggested heavy-handedly. The others shrugged, Bill unwillingly, Philip still smouldering and Geoff amused.

The mood had deteriorated too far for the rest of the meal to be a success. Instead of being able to relax, as the host I had to make an effort and was only too pleased when they all, except Sunil, eventually left. Then Philip and his ghost were forgotten in the tense hope of a new affair and balancing of long-term aspirations against immediate sexual hunger. We lingered over the washing-up, talking about work and finding mutual interests where none had existed before. Then there was coffee and as darkness fell I debated inviting him to stay but he said he had to go.

I was still awake when the telephone rang after midnight. Annoyed, I tried to ignore it, but it persisted and in the end I picked up the receiver.

"Nick? It's Philip. Can you help me? Please?" He sounded

distressed, but I had heard these tones before.

"What is it?"

"I'm in Cockfosters and I've got no money, either on me or at home. If I take a cab to your place, will you pay for it, please?"

"Well," I hesitated, "yes, if I must. How long will you be?"

"I don't know. Thirty minutes? An hour?"

I wasn't going to stay awake that long. "You know where the key is, don't you," — under a loose stone — "I'll leave twenty pounds on the hall table. You can pay me back tomorrow. Just don't wake me."

"I won't. Thanks terribly. Good . . ."

"Hold it," I said, before he could put down the receiver. "What are you doing in Cockfosters? I thought the place only existed on tube maps."

"It doesn't matter."

"Come on. I do you a favour, you do me one. Where've you been?"

"I saw him again." He spoke in a mixture of reluctance and defiance.

"Who? Not the man you were talking about?"

"I followed him out here on the last train."

"And didn't you speak to him?"

"He vanished again."

"What do you mean, vanished?"

"Just that. He was the only other person in the carriage and when I got out there was no one there. I was going to speak to him but he signalled me to wait. He really is attractive, Nick. And he wants me, I know he does."

"How? What do you mean?"

"It's the way he looks at me. He . . . Oh, forget it, I can't explain. Thanks for the money. I'll give it back to you tomorrow." The line went dead.

I should have stayed up, but I was tired and preferred to think about Sunil and what he might mean to me rather than ponder over Philip's weird obsession. So I left the money in the hall, came back to bed and was soon asleep.

Two ten-pound notes were returned the next day before I

came home from college. Beside them lay a short note. "Many thanks. I've seen him again and we almost spoke. I'll try and bring him round in the next day or two." Not sure whether to take the message seriously, I called Philip, but there was no reply.

That day had seen the start of a particularly busy week and my free time for the next few evenings was mortgaged by preparation and correction. I phoned Philip every evening and let it ring for some time before putting the receiver down and punching Sunil's number. His schedule was also busy, but he was happy to spare the time to talk. I knew there was a great difference between his laissez-faire attitude and my cut-and-dried ways, but he seemed as quietly eager as myself to slowly bridge the gap between us.

I would not admit to myself the unease that took me over to Philip's flat on Thursday evening, only a curiosity to find out why he had not called. It disturbed me to see that his home was in worse than its usual cluttered state — dirty dishes were piled up in the kitchen and unwashed clothes were scattered here and there. I left a note for him and waited at home all night hoping he would call. When I phoned his work the next day, I discovered he had not been in since Monday; nor did any other friends I called have any other word.

The police on Friday evening were unhelpful but not obstructive. After muttering something about next of kin, they took down such information as I could give and made no reassuring remarks about Philip's being found or turning up. Alone at home, ugly visions crossed my mind — he was in some hospital with amnesia, had got in trouble with some criminals, had been slaughtered by a madman with a knife. I shuddered and turned to the television for relief.

Sunil arrived the next morning. He stood in the kitchen as I boiled water for coffee, distracting me with the invitation of a clean white shirt lazily covering smooth brown skin. I was about to mention Philip, but it was Sunil who brought up his name, saying he had seen him twice during the week.

"Where?" I turned, almost scalding myself with the kettle.

"On the tube, of all places."

"Are you serious?"

"Yes." Sunil was puzzled at my response. "He was with some other guy. Tall, German-looking, quite sexy. He smiled at me and I went over to speak to them, but they got out before I did. Quite a coincidence, isn't it?"

"Yes," I said, not sure why I felt less relieved than afraid.

"You know," Sunil went on, smiling with a strange, almost conspiratorial look. "I've got a feeling I'm going to run into them again soon."

SIMON'S DINNER PARTY

I was thinking of going to the cinema but didn't fancy going on my own, when Richard phoned up with Simon's invitation. Two hundred pounds if I'd go to his dinner party and stay the night — and no extras if I didn't want to. I wasn't sure I believed Richard, especially when talking about that amount of money, but he said I'd seen Simon a couple of weeks before and made such an impression that he was desperate to have me back. I couldn't think who Simon was at first, then I remembered an oldish guy with a round reddish face who lived in a big house in Hampstead; all he'd really wanted was a kiss and a cuddle.

Richard gave me the address again and said he'd been invited too, along with someone called Gary, who worked for him like me but who I hadn't met before. There were going to be two or three others there as well, friends of Simon's that Richard didn't know. It'd be a lot more pleasant than the usual jobs, he told me, and the money was certainly nothing to sneeze at.

Two hundred pounds, I thought as I lay in the bath. Half of it would go straight into the bank and the rest . . . I'd probably buy a couple of shirts and tapes and a meal out and the money would be gone. It sounded like a lot but it wasn't. Well, maybe there'd be another Simon along soon.

I took my time dressing, as I always do. I always check I'm not putting on weight and there're no spots on my skin. I'm proud of my body — I go to dance classes twice a week to keep in shape.

I keep thinking I ought to go to auditions, take up dancing as a
career, but I never have time — there's always a job to go to or I
wake up late. Maybe one day. Anyway, that evening I dressed all
in white because it was summer and it went well with my tan. I
thought I looked really good and told myself Simon couldn't
complain he wasn't getting his money's worth.

It was warm enough to drive across town with the windows
open. There wasn't much traffic, but I went slowly anyway, as if
I was on holiday and had all the time in the world. I wished I was
on holiday, in fact. London was all right but it was a pain not to
be able to go away whenever I wanted to. Maybe by August I'd
have enough money to go to Key West. Richard went every year
and said it was much better than Mykonos or Ibiza. It sounded
like fun and maybe I'd meet some rich American there that I
really liked.

Simon's house had a garden and a porch and ivy growing up
the wall. I've been in a lot of nice houses, but I remembered that
his was one of the nicest. The rooms I'd seen were large and
beautifully decorated and had old, comfortable furniture and
real paintings hanging on the walls. It was the kind of home I'd
always wanted, instead of the small flat where I lived, where it was
always noisy and all kinds of weirdos shared my front door.

He was just as I remembered him — fat and old and with the
kind of voice that reminds me of officers in old war films. We
shook hands and I gave him a strong, firm grip. He looked me
up and down as if he was inspecting me, but I didn't mind. "Even
more attractive than last time," he said with a big smile. "You
should have come back much sooner. Come in and meet the
others."

I knew Richard, of course, and it was obvious who Gary was
— he had short dark hair and a film star's face and was easily the
handsomest guy in the room. We said hello and I was a bit
disappointed that he did not seem at all interested in me. Peter
and Charles were both much older, probably about forty.
Charles seemed quite friendly and ordinary, but Peter had a
moustache and looked like the kind of man who's always lifting
weights in the gym.

I sat down while Simon got me a drink. Richard asked if I was still having problems with the car and Peter asked me what kind I had. I told him it was a Volkswagen and he pretended to be interested, but I don't think he was. Then Simon handed me my glass and sat next to me and started talking as if we were old friends. I didn't mind that, except I couldn't remember anything about him apart from the fact that I thought he worked in insurance. That didn't seem to bother him; he just put his hand on my knee and chatted away, asking me all sorts of questions about what I'd been doing. Richard always tells me not to talk about other clients, because they like to pretend you're doing it just for them, so I didn't really know what to say. I told him about the dance classes and made it sound as if I spent all my time there and he said it was a pity he didn't know the kind of people who might be able to give me a job.

By the time we all had a second drink I was really quite relaxed. Simon wasn't just talking to me and everyone else was joining in. Only Gary was a bit shy; I kept wishing he'd look at me a bit more often, show he fancied me. I hoped I was his type and I tried to look as if I was bigger than I was in case he preferred guys with muscles. Then I thought that maybe he did like me and just wasn't showing it — after all we weren't being paid to come to someone else's party to cruise each other. I wondered who he'd end up with. Probably Peter, although I hoped it would be Charles.

Wouldn't it be nice to live like this, I thought as we all went through to the dining-room. The table was beautifully set out with candles and silver and the chairs around it were the kind that look as if they'd break the moment you sat on them but are really old and valuable. Richard whistled and Simon looked pleased. He had us all sit down in particular places — I was next to him and had Peter on my right — then he poured out wine and went to get the soup. It was cold but tasted really good, just like the rest of the food. It sort of surprised me and made me envious that Simon could cook, because all I can do is boil an egg and open packets and cans.

We talked about all sorts of things — holidays and politics and

opera at first, then, as always happens, we got on to sex. Peter
told us stories about when he'd lived in the States and Simon told
us about goings-on when he'd been at school, which must have
been a long time ago. Of course someone mentioned Aids, but
that was too depressing and pretty soon Richard made us change
the subject.

There was another kind of wine with the meat and when that
ran out we opened another. Simon seemed to like me a lot. He
put his hand on my leg and asked me all sorts of questions, which
was nice, but also embarrassing, the questions, I mean. He
wanted to know about my family and the kinds of jobs I'd had
and I didn't know what to say. I don't like talking about the time
before I came to London, because I think it's unlucky and if
things go wrong I'll end up back home again. And I haven't
worked much, not since I left school. So we got onto dancing
again and I made up this story about auditioning for touring
companies. I said I could be a better dancer if I took more
classes, but I couldn't afford them. It wasn't exactly true, but I
thought it might make him give me a bit more money.

It was when Simon brought in a cake for dessert that it came
out that it was his birthday and he was having this party to
celebrate. It was a bit embarrassing because no one else seemed
to have known. Charles proposed a toast with a new bottle of
wine and we all wished him many happy returns. Richard asked
how old he was and Simon said he'd have to admit he was fifty-
seven. I thought it was a bit odd having people like Gary and me
over on a day like that but I suppose he wanted to give himself
a present. Or maybe Peter and Charles were paying, but that
didn't seem likely and I didn't like to ask.

While the others were having coffee, Simon showed me
round the house. It was as nice as I remembered it from last time.
He had lots of rooms; what he called a drawing-room and a study
with a computer and other machines. The kitchen had all the
gadgets you'd ever need to cook the most fantastic meal, not that
I'd know how to use them. Then he showed me his collection of
toby jugs, which he was very proud of and said that some of the
furniture he had was made by people who were famous,

although I'd never heard of them. All the time he had his arm round my shoulder and kept telling me that he could see I really appreciated such things even if I didn't know much about them. I didn't believe him, because he'd been drinking, but it was nice of him to say it. "You know I've really missed you," he said when we were in his bedroom, "you should have come back sooner." "Yeah, well," I said, "you can phone Richard anytime, because I'm usually available." I didn't like reminding him that he had to pay, but there was nothing else I could say. "Well, at least you're staying tonight," he went on. "We can talk about that later." "Sure," I said, although I wasn't sure what he meant.

We went down to the television room, where the others were watching the beginning of a porn film. All the furniture had been cleared out and the floor was covered with sheets and cushions. There was a radiator on and a small table with KY, poppers and condoms. The others had begun to take off their clothes. Peter and Richard were kissing hard but Charles and Gary were a bit more shy. Gary had his shirt off — he had a really nice tanned body and I hoped I'd be able to touch it later. But Simon was leaning over me and I knew I really ought to be doing everything with him.

I let him take off my clothes and hoped he didn't crease them as he put them away. He was a bit clumsy and not very good at kissing or stroking and I didn't like his bad breath. I thought I'd better do something, so I took off his shirt and trousers and saw how pale and flabby his skin was, like most of the clients I get. Luckily he didn't expect me to do much, so I just lay back with my eyes closed. After a time I felt another pair of hands on my legs. It was Richard. Then it was pretty much free for all for a time. I managed to get hold of Gary a couple of times but it was obvious he wasn't as interested in me as I was in him. That depressed me, but I thought, well, I'm really here for the money, so I went back to Simon, who hadn't really joined in.

After that it was pretty much couples. Richard and Peter were being very athletic, as if they were trying to beat some kind of record. Charles and Gary were more gentle and romantic. I let Simon do whatever he wanted, which wasn't much, and I was careful not to come, because I was sure he would want me to later in the night. He started muttering things like he loved me and when he came, he panted and went all red and called me darling, which I didn't much like. Pretty soon everyone was finished and we wiped ourselves dry. Then Simon switched off the TV and offered us more coffee and drinks in the living-room.

When we were all sitting down again the atmosphere didn't seem as friendly as it had done before. Richard was as chatty as he always is, but Gary looked bored and Peter and Charles seemed in a hurry to go home. I felt quite sorry for Simon because he was doing his best to be cheerful and after all it was his birthday. When Peter said he had to go, the others stood up as well. Charles offered Gary a lift, which he accepted, and we all walked to the door. I felt kind of funny as I stood behind Simon and watched everyone leave; it was as if the house was as much mine as his and they'd been my guests as well. Richard told me to phone him the next day — I was sure it was to tell him exactly how much I had earned — and I politely said goodbye to the rest. Then Simon closed the door and we were alone.

"We don't need to go to bed right away, do we?" he asked, but he was as much telling me what he'd decided as asking me what I wanted to do. So we went back to the living-room and he poured us out another drink.

"If I'd known it was your birthday, I'd have brought you a present," I said when he had poured us another drink and we were sitting down again.

"What? Oh yes. Well, I'm getting too old for that sort of thing," he replied.

"No, you're not," I told him, because that's what you have to say.

He didn't say anything, but sat there looking sad and bleary-eyed and I began to feel a bit uncomfortable. So I looked around and saw a picture of a fox hunt and asked him about it just to keep the conversation going. He told me he used to go when he was younger and lived in the country with his parents. Then he didn't say anything and I sat with my glass in my hand, not really wanting another drink and not knowing what to say.

"Do you like coming here?" he asked suddenly. "Yes," was the only thing I could say. "Would you like to come here more often?" he went on. "If you invite me . . ." I said, sort of leaving the question of money hanging in the air. He didn't say anything for a minute. "You're not like the others," he said. "You're not just interested in the money, in getting it over with quickly in order to leave." "Well, that's not polite, is it?" I said, feeling a bit guilty, because often I did just want to get it over with so I could leave.

"You know, I'm really fond of you." He wasn't looking at me and I wondered if he was as embarrassed as I was. "You could stay here, you know, if you liked." "You mean tonight," I asked. "No, not just tonight, for as long as you wanted."

Wow, I thought. Live here, in this nice house and have Simon cook for me and everything. I wouldn't have to work for Richard any more. I could do what I wanted; it'd be great. But then I thought about living and sleeping with Simon and how old he was and all the things he'd expect me to do. It wasn't him I wanted to be with, but someone I could love, who was my age and handsome and had a wonderful body. Surely love was more important than money?

Simon emptied his glass and reached for the bottle. I thought he'd drunk a lot but he didn't seem drunk. "You could do whatever you liked," he said. "I wouldn't want you to give up your friends or anything like that. And you wouldn't need to work for Richard any more. A boy like you shouldn't be doing that."

But I like working for Richard, I almost said. I get to meet all kinds of people and maybe one day I'll . . . Then I realised that this is what I'd been doing it for, to meet someone who really liked me. Only I'd imagined it differently. I didn't think it'd be someone like Simon. I thought he'd be younger and suntanned and good-looking, like Gary, and he'd have a house in the country and a swimming-pool and all that sort of thing.

"Well?" Simon asked, topping up my glass. I didn't really want it, but it would have been rude to refuse.

"It's very kind of you," I said, because I had to say something.

"But are you sure that I wouldn't be in your way?"

"What do you mean, 'in my way'?" He laughed and moved closer so that he was sitting right beside me. I could smell his breath again and see how big his face was and how thick the skin. "I need someone. I can't live alone. We're not meant to live alone, are we? It's a cold world; we all need someone to care for. Don't you agree?"

"Yes," I said, because what he was saying was true. I was trying to think what I'd get and what I'd have to give up if I lived with Simon, but it was difficult to concentrate because his hand was gripping my leg.

"You don't have to tell me now," he said. "You can tell me in the morning. But I hope you'll say yes." He leaned over and kissed me and put his arm around me. It was a bit uncomfortable because he was heavy and leaning on me, but I kissed him back anyway. He pushed his tongue between my teeth and I realised that when you're kissing someone that close you don't notice whether they've got bad breath. He put his hand between my legs and I was worried because I wasn't excited but he didn't seem to mind.

"Come on." he said, sitting up and patting my knee. "Let's go to bed."

While he was in the bathroom I sat on the bed and looked at the pictures on the walls and felt how thick the carpet was and I thought that maybe it wouldn't be so bad living there. Some people I knew would think me an idiot if I didn't take the chance. It wasn't as if there was anything funny about Simon and I wouldn't have to do much to keep him happy. Then he came in and I went and washed all over and used the toothbrush he'd left out for me.

When I came back he was already in bed. I got in and the sheets were stiff and clean and smelled nice, like the hotel I'd stayed in once when I was young. This would be great every night, I thought, and I cuddled up to Simon feeling warm and comfortable thinking about it. He finished off his drink and took a couple of pills and we hugged and kissed for a bit. "Yeah, I'd like to stay," I whispered into his ear. "Good," he said, but he didn't seem to be paying much attention, because a minute later he said he was tired and switched off the light.

I said goodnight and lay on my side like I always do and tried to get to sleep. I couldn't for a while, though, because I was thinking about all the things I could do if I lived with Simon. I could meet him for tea at the Ritz or learn to cook so that he could have all his friends round. And I could invite all the people I knew from the dance classes and they'd be really impressed. I might even be able to have Gary over when Simon was out. He'd be bound to be interested in me when he saw where I was living. So I told myself I really would accept and fell asleep thinking how great everything would be.

The next morning it was a bit of a shock to be woken by the alarm at seven o'clock. I'd had some nice dreams about Gary and money and wanted to lie in but Simon said I had to get up because he had to go to work.

"Do I have to get up now?" I asked. I thought that if I was going to live there it would be nice to spend the rest of the day in bed or just looking around the house.

"I'm afraid you do," Simon said, his voice all different, like an army colonel and not the friendly old man he'd been the night before. "I have to leave soon and I can't leave you alone in the house."

"Why not? You told me last night I could stay as long as I wanted." I sat up with the sheets around my waist. He looked silly standing there with no clothes on and a big hairy pot-belly.

"Did I?" He didn't seem to understand for a minute. "Well, we both had a lot to drink last night. I didn't mean you could move straight in. We have to get to know each other first. After all, I don't know anything about you."

"Yes, you do. I told you all about myself."

"Well, that's as maybe. Now, will you get up?"

I didn't know what to say. I felt cheated and angry because all the nice things I could see around me which I had thought were mine didn't belong to me anymore. I wanted to say something to show him that he was wrong and he should let me stay, but I couldn't think clearly with him standing there waiting for me to move. He watched as I got dressed as if he thought that I'd steal something if he was out of the room. Then we went downstairs to the kitchen and had some orange juice and coffee. He seemed a bit more relaxed then and I asked him when he wanted me to come back. "What for?" he asked. "To get to know each other," I said, but I could see he didn't really want to. "I'll give Richard a call," he said and I wondered whether to give him my own number but I knew Richard wouldn't give me any more jobs if he found out.

I had a look round when Simon went to get his coat and briefcase and made it really obvious that I hadn't stolen anything when he returned. It was really a nice house and so warm and comfortable and when I thought it had nearly been mine I nearly cried. He was going to drop me off at the tube station until I reminded him I had my own car. As we were leaving, he handed me an envelope which I stuffed in my pocket. He didn't say thank you or when he would call. Fuck you, I thought, as I got into the car and drove away.

Of course it was the rush hour and it took me ages to get home. When I was stuck at one of the lights I opened the envelope and saw there was only one hundred pounds in it. That made me so angry that the minute I got in I phoned Richard. He wasn't pleased to be woken up and when I told him about the money he claimed that Simon had only said he might pay two hundred. I didn't know who to blame, but I knew I couldn't get mad at Richard or he wouldn't give me any more jobs. So I said I was sorry for waking him and put down the phone. I was really unhappy because I'd lost both Simon and Gary and I didn't think I'd meet anyone like either of them for a long time.

THE
BENEFACTOR

You've been here before, haven't you? We're south of the
Thames on a Friday evening, in a pub where the music is loud
and the clientele gay. You probably know these three standing
with their backs to the bar. They're in their twenties, single and
solvent. There's Steve, all five foot six of him, sells jewellery in
Bond Street and dreams of the day when a young and handsome
millionaire will walk in and sweep him off his feet. The tall one's
Adrian, tired after ten hours hunting down a computer virus that
insisted on giving each of a bank's customers several thousand
pounds; a little older than Steve, he's successful at work but
haunted by the suspicion that life is passing him by. Lastly,
there's Derek, whose resemblance to the boy in the latest Levi's
ad is more than coincidence; he's just been made manager of a
pizza restaurant and he's been calculating, with the help of a few
drinks, how long it will take him to start his own chain.

This gathering is a weekly ritual, an opportunity for each to
unwind. They arrive here about eight and after a couple of hours
drift apart to pursue their separate fantasies. In the meantime
they talk, as tonight, about men. Partly because it's all they have
in common, but mostly because the topic is endless and never
dull. This evening they have rated all of those around them, with
some humour, little generosity and even less discretion. Yet
somehow they have missed the most imposing figure, the one
who stands, without a glass, a few feet away. He's middle-aged,
dressed in a black that is more anonymous than a uniform, and

for the last few minutes has been staring at them intently.

Most young men would allow him one glance before dismissing him as yet another individual who offers money rather than looks, connections rather than charisma. But those who looked closer would see in his dark eyes, strong cheeks and the firm set of his mouth an expression they did not recognise, one that both attracted and made them afraid. Steve, however, does not notice such details, is aware only that he is being watched and, with the belligerence that has become his second nature, wants to know why. "Which one of us do you fancy then?" he leans across to ask.

"None of you." The man smiles without embarrassment.

"So what do you want?"

"Nothing."

"So why are you staring?" Derek and Adrian interrupt their conversation, turn their attention to the stranger.

"I was curious, that was all. I thought I might be able to offer you something." The man's voice is quiet, deep and accentless. He has joined them without being invited, stands oblivious to Adrian's raised eyebrows and Steve's hostile stare.

"What are you selling?" Derek asks, "Soap powder or religion?"

"I'm not selling anything. I'm offering you. Whatever you want."

"Whatever we want?" Steve laughs. "A million pounds. In used ten pound notes."

"I'm sorry." The stranger seems genuinely apologetic. "That's too general. Try something more personal."

"Such as?" Derek asks.

"Something like wisdom, strength, long life." The man stands perfectly serious, perfectly relaxed, as if he were discussing no more than the weather.

"And you'll give them to us?" Adrian speaks at last.

The man nods. Steve suppresses a snort, Derek a smile.

"We each get three wishes, I suppose." Adrian again.

"I'm afraid not. Just one."

"I love it," Derek finally laughs. "A godmother for three fairies."

The stranger frowns, in disagreement rather than anger. "I prefer the term benefactor." Steve mutters something under his breath, but Derek, amused, allows himself to think aloud. "If *I* had a wish," he says, "I'd want the hunky number at the petrol station to seduce me. Not to turn gay, just to want me and no one else."

"And you?" the man asks Steve.

Steve searches for a put-down, but finds himself thinking instead. "I'd want a Rolls." The stranger shakes his head. "You can't do that? Then I'd want to be tall. Tall and handsome and have everyone fall for me."

Now the game has begun it is Adrian's turn. "This is ridiculous," he says, "but if you want me to say something, I'd want . . . I'd want to be truly, desperately, head over heels in love."

There is a moment's silence against the hubbub of the bar.

"Well," says Steve to the stranger. "I'm still the same height. What went wrong?"

"Tell me again." And Steve finds himself staring into the man's eyes as if hypnotised, hears his own voice slow and deep and far away. "I want to be tall and handsome and have *everyone* fall for me."

He feels odd, as if he's drunk too much and the room can't decide whether to stand still or spin round. He closes his eyes, takes a breath, opens them again and feels better but still strange. Adrian and Derek are chattering away, but he hasn't been paying attention to what they're saying. Putting down his drink, he says he's going for a piss. As he walks off, for some reason he's aware of his height — his legs and the ground seem a long way away and he's not used to being face to face with people and having them look back. He moves slowly, trying to work out what is wrong. A tall thin guy with a drooping moustache is staring at him; to cover his uncertainty, Steve winks as he passes and almost laughs as the other's expression changes abruptly to surprise.

In the toilet he inspects his face in the mirror. He doesn't look sick but. . . has he always been that good-looking? His nose has shrunk, his hair's come forward and something's happened to his jaw and mouth. He looks like a popstar, no, a model, one of those incredibly handsome young men in fashion magazines that you never see in real life. The blond hair, the blue eyes and strong cheeks; he's always fancied guys like that, guys who look cool and rich, who look as if they've got everything made. "You're really something," he whispers to his reflection, "really . . ."

The door opens and Steve jerks back embarrassed. It's the man with the moustache, who comes over, stands beside him and pretends to wash his hands. Their eyes meet in the mirror, the stranger's expression is one that Steve does not recognise. To give him time to understand it, he takes out his comb and pulls it slowly through his hair. The other man watches him with eyes of expectancy and fear. He wants me, Steve realises, he's desperate; I've only got to say come and he'll follow me home like a dog. Flattered, he is about to respond, but he sees the lines of age and failure in the man's face and remembers there are many others in the bar. And tonight, he is suddenly certain he can pick anyone he wants. "Nice try," he tells his admirer, "but not good enough," and with an unwonted spring in his step he turns and leaves, as cocky as the day he made his first thousand pound sale.

He was with some people, wasn't he? It seems a long time ago and he doesn't want to go back. Besides, he can see better what's available when he's on his own. With another drink in hand he stands by the door and looks over the familiar scene. He seems to tower above it now, whereas before it always used to dominate him. He can look round at leisure, pick out the best available. There are indeed some presentable guys although none is as attractive as the image of himself he has just seen. But if the worst comes to the worst, by the window there's a flattop with earrings and a cheeky grin, on the left a guy in training pants with a knowing expression and not far away a young blond in T-shirt and faded jeans. Tonight, at least, he won't go home alone.

Quite a few are watching him. Some slowly sweep their eyes casually from wall to wall, lingering on him for longer than chance would allow. Others stare quite openly. Even those who are with friends or lovers or whose backs are to him are aware of his presence, look round every so often to check that he has not gone. And in everyone's eyes, whether masked by disinterest, idle curiosity or no disguise at all, lies the same strong desire. They all want me, he tells himself; they're all wondering what chance they've got, what pick-up line would work, what I want to do in bed. I could have them all. I could take them all home, line them up in the hall, have them in one by one and they wouldn't complain. They want me that much.

For a few minutes he is excited, imagines scenes of intimacy and orgy, but his enthusiasm soon wanes. What's the point, he wonders, if I don't fancy them, if none are as good-looking as me? And how handsome is he really? What did he see in the gents? He wants a mirror in which to check himself, to see that his hair is as wavy, his eyes as deep and his mouth as seductive as he remembers them. There is a mirror on the side wall; to see himself he has to move and as he makes his way across the bar, he is conscious that everyone without exception, whether openly or furtively, is keeping him in view. The attention is like the lightest of caresses, welcome when sought but irritating when imposed. He wants to push it away, to deflect their gaze but does not know how.

The figure in the glass walking towards him makes him stop and catch his breath. Is that really me? Is that tall, handsome guy, the one with the suntan who looks about twenty — or maybe he's much older, there's something about him that's rugged and mature — really Steve Watkins, shop assistant and shrimp-about-town? His memory was wrong; it wasn't good enough. He's perfection personified, everyone's wet dream; no wonder they're all staring, no wonder they all want to speak to him and all lack the nerve to try.

He looks away, afraid to keep watching, afraid the mirror will crack, the spell will break and he will find himself the same, short, unattractive guy he used to be. He turns, bumps into the man behind him, who smiles, says, "My pleasure, my pleasure indeed!"

There is an opening for a conversation there, but the man is too old, losing hair and gaining weight. Steve shrugs, walks away before he has to say something, before he is trapped with words. Everyone seems to be staring at him. He wants to find a dark corner, somewhere he can look out and not be seen, where he can wait like a spider in the corner of her web, but there is nowhere he can hide. The roles are wrong; they should be the prey but he feels like the victim. Damn you, he silently shouts; you can't have me; look away!

He is about to choose someone, anyone, the flattop, the guy at the fruit machine. He'll say "Let's go" and they'll come at once; out in the street he'll be able to breathe. But the door has opened and a man has come in, is waiting to be served on the other side of the bar. He is easily more desirable than any of the others — six foot tall, dark hair, laughing blue eyes and a strong and pleasant smile. Steve has talked to him before, looked up into the clouds at that god-like face and suggested he take him home. Then the offer was gently refused but tonight, Steve knows, is different, tonight no invitation he makes will be turned down. Brushing past bodies and faces, he hurries round, greets the other as he picks up his drink, asks with an attempted smile, "Remember me?"

"I . . ."

"I'm Steve. Your name's Ross."

Ross nods in acknowledgement, curious and flattered.

"Are you on your own?" Steve goes on, adding, "So am I."

"I'm surprised," Ross says. "Are you having fun?"

"I will be. In half an hour, with you."

Ross's eyebrows rise. "You seem sure about that."

"I am. Aren't you?"

If Ross hesitates, it is too briefly to be noticed. "Do I have time to finish my drink?"

"No." The word is curt and flat.

Ross looks with mock regret at his still full glass, shrugs and puts it down.

It is a relief to be shielded by the darkness of the street, to be walking towards his car with only Ross's eyes on him. Ross sits in the passenger seat, puts his hand on Steve's knee as Steve adjusts the mirror so that he can see both himself and the road behind. His reflection is no longer a surprise but a promise of dreams to be fulfilled.

They talk, but Steve is aware of little more than the road and the urgent desire to get home. His flat is near and soon they are inside, closing the door and urgently holding, kissing and undressing each other, tripping over trousers and shoes as Steve leads them into the bedroom. Ross's body emerges lean and hard but with little definition; Steve looks down and sees the perfect curves of his own muscles.

"You're quite something," Ross tells him, as they draw apart to remove the last articles of clothing.

"I suppose I am," Steve says and lies back on the bed, eyes closed, conscious of Ross standing there, admiring him, looking carefully, fruitlessly, for some imperfection.

He feels the weight of Ross straddling him, bending over to kiss and stroke him. For a moment he cannot remember what to do, then he opens his eyes, reaches out and pulls Ross to him. They kiss, bodies tight against each other, until Ross breaks and pulls back to stare at Steve again and let his hand glide over the contours of his body.

Steve looks at Ross, at himself and back at Ross. Something is missing. He kisses Ross absently and lets his hand wander between Ross's legs. Then abruptly he stands up. "Just a minute," he says, going out into the hall.

To Ross's amusement Steve comes back with a full-length mirror, which he places in the corner of the bed where it meets the wall. He lies down, invites Ross onto him. They hold each other for a moment and hands begin to explore again, until Steve, looking at the mirror over Ross's shoulder, realises that he cannot see himself, only an undistinguishable part of Ross's back. He sits up again, unaware of Ross's surprise, and moves the mirror again. "Happy?" Ross asks, but Steve barely hears the question as he tries to shift them into a position that will satisfy him.

Only when it is hanging over them, Steve realises, will he see himself full-length. For that he needs string. He gets up again, goes through to the kitchen and looks through several drawers.

"Are you going to be long?" Ross's voice is thick with sarcasm as Steve takes down pictures and ties the mirror diagonally across the corner of the wall.

"No," Steve tells him, distracted by the reflection of his own thighs, his cock, the ripples of his stomach. But the string is not long enough and he has to look for more. When he returns Ross has started to dress. There is no more than a moment's disappointment and it is only politeness that makes him ask, "Aren't you going to stay?"

"Only if you stop playing with the mirror," Ross tells him calmly as he slips on his shoes and pulls on his shirt. Steve adds the extra string, slackens the tension to achieve the appropriate angle, ties a knot and leans back to check that his whole body is in view. When at last he looks round he is alone.

Lying back on the bed, he stares up at his reflection, following the sweep of his leg up to his groin, across the valley of his stomach and over the twin peaks of his chest. At last he arrives at his face, his perfect face. There is the mouth that is both yielding and hard, the angular cheeks of youth and strength, the defenceless eyes that both promise and protect. He remembers a long, long time ago that he wanted to be tall and handsome and have everyone fall for him. His wish has been granted; no one, not even himself, can resist. Putting out a hand, he slowly reaches up, hoping, praying, that he can penetrate the glass and make love with the only body he will ever again want.

* * *

Derek is a little surprised to see Steve leave so abruptly, but he turns back to the stranger and asks, "Well, what about me?"

"Your wish?"

"Yes."

"Tell me again what you want."

Derek sees a face that is kind yet distant and thinks that he has nothing to lose by humouring him. He starts to speak, finds himself intoning the words as if they were a prayer. "I want the number who works at the petrol station across the road, the hunky one with the two gold ear-rings, to fall in love with me. Not to turn gay, just to want me."

He was late. His first day as manager and he was going to be late. He knew he shouldn't have got drunk last night. There was that strange guy and Steve had gone off suddenly and after that he couldn't remember much. Where were those new shoe-laces he had bought? On the floor. Bending down gave him a headache. Next time he'd wash it out with a gallon of water before he went to bed, not after he got up. Got them. Check trousers, no grease stains. Thank God he'd ironed his shirt the night before. Keys, pen, spare shirt, wallet. Right. Check himself in the mirror. Not bad. James Dean, eat your heart out. Downstairs, out into the Mini, switch on, check the petrol. Damn, nearly empty.

He looked across the road, saw that the garage was quiet. It was early on Saturday morning and most of the world was still in bed. With a loud zoom he made a U-turn into the forecourt, got out, pumped a tenner's worth of unleaded and strode over to pay. God, it was him again. The Hackney Hunk, the East End Idol. Derek didn't know what, but something about this guy made him go weak at the knees, soft in the head, stiff in the . . . And of course the guy was straight as the proverbial die, winked at every woman and called her darling, had frozen into contempt the day Derek had playfully winked back. He was living proof that God did not exist, for no compassionate God would have created such a dream and kept him so tantalisingly out of Derek's reach.

In the shop the young man took the twenty-pound note and punched the till. "How are you, then?"

"Huh?" said Derek, taken aback by the pleasant tone.

"How are you? Haven't seen you for a couple of days." He handed Derek his change, gazed at him with dark green eyes.

"Fine," Derek replied warily, "just fine."

"You busy this evening?"

"Huh?" Had he heard what he thought?

"You want to drop by about six? I get off then. We can go for a drink."

"A drink?" Just the two of them? Derek saw himself taking advantage of a very drunk and very desirable garage hand.

"Yeah, a drink."

The vision faltered, was replaced by the nightmare of an ambush, of being beaten up by a group of the youth's mocking friends. "I don't think I can make it."

"How about tomorrrow? I could drop by in the afternoon."

"I'm working." Edge restored to his voice and decision to his legs, Derek turned and walked out before he was tempted into something he couldn't handle. What a pity, he thought, all that beautiful flesh going to waste. But some risks weren't worth it and leopards never did change their spots.

It was not until late that evening that Derek, tired but satisfied, persuaded himself that Supa-Pizza could do without him for a few hours at least. The next day, Sunday, he was not due in till the evening. After a late and lazy breakfast he was about to go out in the expectation of meeting Steve and Adrian at the pub, when the doorbell rang and a few moments later he heard Robert, his flatmate, tell the unknown visitor, "he's in there."

"What the. . . ?" Derek said as his bedroom door opened and the boy from the garage walked in.

"I saw your car, thought you'd be in."

"But how did you know I lived here? There're half a dozen flats in the building."

"I just knocked at a couple of doors, asked if the geezer with the blue Mini lived here. Your friend said yes. Right little bender, isn't he?"

"I'm a bender too," Derek said, his anger rising. "And I don't like the word."

"Sorry," the boy said, not sounding sorry at all. "Anyway, it's you I came to see. What's your name? Mine's Dean."

"Derek," Derek said, the anger swiftly melting in the proximity of Dean's muscles and smile.

"You want a drink? I brought some beer with me." Dean held up a plastic bag, sat down before his host could object. I don't believe this, Derek told himself. Is he here to get me drunk and do me over or to come out of the closet? No, he's not gay; he's too cocky, got nothing to hide.

But he was not one to refuse a can of lager and, with Derek on the bed and Dean on the only chair, a stilted conversation began. It was not long, however, before the alcohol helped them discover the common problems of running a pizza parlour and a garage, a Mini and a BMW. First Dean and then Derek slumped to the floor, their legs apart and idling against each other.

"Just why did you come to see me?" Derek asked when they had come to the end of their experience of silencers and exhausts.

"Dunno. I just thought you were a nice guy." As Dean spoke, his hand rose in a gesture, fell on Derek's knee where it lay in thick silence.

I'm going to get thumped; I hope to God Robert hears me scream. Stifling the thought, Derek reached over to kiss Dean and was greeted by eagerness rather than violence, by Dean's probing tongue and gripping hands.

"You've done that before," Derek accused some time later as they lay back, naked and exhausted, on the bed.

"What? This? No way." Dean was adamant. "I told you, I'm not queer."

"Well, I'm no woman. And you did things no straight man ever would."

"Maybe," Dean shrugged, "but you're different."

Stop trying to kid yourself, Derek was about to protest when Dean interrupted him. "Can we do it again?"

"Now?" He couldn't; or perhaps he could . . .

It took Derek several weeks to accept that his new lover was not lying, that he never had been and never would be gay. It was not merely the talk of girlfriends and the habit of pointing out attractive women in the street; everything about Dean identified him as straight. His body was thickset, sported tattoos on each arm and released a sweat that tasted faintly of fried eggs. His clothes were shapeless and of every clashing colour. His vocabulary overflowed with four-letter words, his accent was authentic

Cockney and his values centred happily on football and page
three of the *Sun*.

Yet several times a week he knocked on Derek's door in the
early evening or late at night, occasionally drunk, more often
sober, almost apologetic at the intrusion. They would sit and
talk, sometimes for hours, before making love and falling asleep,
arms across each other protectively. Once accustomed to the
situation, Derek saw no reason to object. Indeed, Dean seemed
more masculine, more real than the opera-loving men with neat
moustaches that he came across in bars and more honest than
the self-centred young men in the few relationships that he had
had. If Dean had flaws, not least his contempt for "queers", they
could be worked on; in the meantime Derek's only fear was that
soon — and probably in the middle of their most energetic sex
— Dean would suddenly come out with "What the fuck am I
doing?" and storm off, slamming doors and smashing break-
ables as he went.

Instead Dean asked, "Why don't I move in?"

"What?"

"You heard. Why don't I move in? We could be together all
the time, except when we was at work. It'd save you money. I'd
pay half your rent."

"There's not enough room for three of us."

"Then give Robert the heave. He doesn't like me anyway."

"Robert's an old friend. I'm not going to tell him to leave." But
by chance or design Robert announced that he was moving out
to a flat much nearer his work. Without waiting for permission,
Dean moved in his stereo system, his collection of stolen
roadway signs and two hundred videotapes. Derek wanted to
protest but found he couldn't; the old suspicion that he was
being duped, that one night he would find himself beaten up and
the flat stripped of its few valuables, silenced by a constant
hunger for Dean's company, for his body.

For several weeks there were no problems. They planned
their shifts to coincide and spent evenings discovering shared
tastes at the cinema, in pubs and concerts. If staying in, whoever
arrived first would cook for the other, Derek creating exotic

dishes from a cookbook, Dean opening cans or following the instructions on frozen food packets. An evening would follow of talk or television and if they fell asleep before making love, next morning they would often fulfil the wish of the night before. They were only rarely apart, when Dean, almost reluctantly, would go out with some old mates or a girlfriend he had known months before. Derek acquiesced, even encouraged such excursions, for they proved that Dean was indeed the straight man that he claimed to be.

In time, however, the dream began to fade. Derek began to resent the time Dean spent in keeping the flat clean and dust-free. He had no sympathy when he came home to find Dean upset because the recipe he was trying was having no success. He felt betrayed when Dean suggested they spend an hour in the local gay bar. The macho man was turning soft, the straight man was becoming gay. This was not what Derek wanted, a lover like all the rest. He tried to stop the process, mocking the changes that Dean was offering him, but Dean, lacking understanding, only tried harder to please.

One wet autumn evening he turned up at the restaurant at the end of Derek's shift, waited impatiently at the door while his lover checked the till. "That's a wonderful greeting," he said, when Derek eventually closed the door.

"I thought you were going out. With Amanda or whatever-her-name-is."

"Her? I can see her any time. She just wants a bit on the side."

"And don't you? You're becoming as queer as I am."

"Crap. You're the only man I want. Otherwise give me a bird every time. Anyway, what's wrong with being gay? That's what you're always on at me about."

"Nothing," Derek said as they walked towards the car. "But I don't want you to be."

"Quite the little hypocrite, aren't you?" Dean's tone was suddenly harsh.

"What do you mean?"

"You want me to be something special, don't you? You want to have something that no one else, no gay guy can have. As long as I'm screwing girls you want me. Otherwise you don't care; you'd kick me out tomorrow. Am I right?"

"That's not true," Derek said, convincing neither himself nor Dean.

"You little bastard. It hasn't got into your thick head that I might be special not because I'm straight, not because of who I fuck, but because I'm me. You don't give a damn about me, the person I am."

"I do." They had stopped by the Mini. Derek heard the violence in Dean's tones, saw it in his frown, in his body's tension. He stood in the road, afraid, unable to move.

"Don't you ever fuck with me, Derek, because no matter how much I love you, I swear I'll kill you."

"You love me?" They had never used the word before.

"Christ, are you that stupid? Do you think I'd be living with you, fucking with you, if I didn't? I don't know what's happened to me. I'm obsessed by you. I can't live without you. My friends and family are beginning to think I've gone queer; I can't explain to them I'm not. The thought of having sex with any other guy makes me sick. I always imagined I'd end up with a wife and lots of kids one day. But I don't want them any more; I want you. For the rest of my life. God knows why. You must have put a spell on me." A vague memory of a strange man in a bar came to Derek and faded away. "Like it or not you're stuck with me," Dean went on. "But you've got to want me for the guy I am, not the part you want me to play. Understand?"

Derek looked at Dean, saw behind the anger the fear of hurt, of being rejected. This wasn't what he wanted, to discover that Dean was no different from any gay man. His lover should be unique, unlike all the rest, a man who was strong, independent, even hostile and contemptuous, not someone vulnerable, someone who needed to love and be loved. His heterosexuality had been a symbol of that strength and now it was on the brink of falling apart.

For a moment Derek thought of telling Dean that it was over, that he had lost interest and did not want to see him again. But he was held back, not only because Dean might attack him in frustration and rage, but because in that moment he began to understand, dimly, the truth of what his lover was saying. From the beginning he had wanted the myth that Dean represented; he had never paid attention to Dean himself. The myth had already shattered, and if Dean too were to go, Derek realised he would lose something which he could never find elsewhere.

The night hung over them; a light rain began. Derek at last found his voice. "Yeah," he nodded, opening the car door, his eyes still on Dean, wary of his anger, love and pain. "I understand." He didn't really, but in time he knew he would.

* * *

Adrian has watched bemused as Steve walks off and Derek falls silent. "Well?" the stranger asks.

"Well what?" Adrian replies, annoyed that his Friday evening, one of the few times in the week when he can properly unwind, has come to such a quick and unexpected end.

"Didn't you say you wanted to be 'truly, desperately, head over heels in love'?"

It is embarrassing to hear his words repeated. "I also want to be stinking rich, to be a black belt in karate and to travel to the moon."

"I can't give you all of those." The man's tone hovers between amusement and regret. Despite his age, late forties, Adrian does not find him unattractive. It's the eyes in particular which fascinate, the expression which he does not quite understand, reminding him of someone he once knew or wanted to know.

"I don't think you can give me any of them, or anything at all."

"No? Look over there."

Adrian follows the man's gaze, sees on the other side of the bar a tall, attractive and familiar figure.

"That's Steve?"

His companion nods.

"Steve!" Adrian calls, suddenly and inexplicably concerned. But his voice is lost in the hubbub and Steve, drink in hand, is already moving away. "Derek. . . " Adrian turns, but Derek too has gone.

"I don't think you'll see them again." The tone is friendly but Adrian is not reassured. "You want to be in love," the stranger goes on, "more than anything else in the world."

"Yes," Adrian says, accepting a situation he can no longer control, "I do."

"Do you know what that means?"

"Of course." He has been near to love many times, with younger men and contemporaries, individuals who slept with him and drank and watched films with him and eventually drifted out of his life. He has glimpsed love, reached for it but always seen it retreat from his grasp, his heart swelling in an emotion that has never been returned or shared.

"I don't think you do. Let me show you."

They had arranged to meet in the cafe at six. Adrian arrived early, taking advantage of the freedom of a Saturday afternoon, and now, three-quarters of an hour later, he was still waiting. Cold coffee cup in hand, he looked out into the street, imagining Patrick ambling along, a tall figure with long coat and trousers flapping around him. He would come in with an embarrassed smile and hang his head in apology. He would sit, mouth a kiss, they would order two more coffees and, eyes glued to each other, knees touching furtively under the table, they would talk and talk and talk.

Adrian did not know whether it was Patrick's looks or person-ality which had attracted him the first night they had met, but now he could no longer distinguish one from the other. His short blond hair stood up in defiance of those around him, while his dark eyes and permanent grin laughed at everyone and everything. His presence threw light, three-dimensionality and vibrancy into a world otherwise dominated by work and routine. It promised something that Adrian did not recognise, but something that he knew he wanted. When with him, Adrian was liberated, alive and amusing; yet at the same time he felt gross, heavy and inadequate, afraid that he was neither interesting nor entertaining enough. Patrick appeared to enjoy his company, laughed with him, shared his bed from time to time, yet in those rare moments that he was honest with himself, Adrian recognised that he was still much further from Patrick's thoughts than Patrick was from his own.

They had known each other for months but still, when alone, Adrian would count the hours, the minutes, the seconds until they next met or spoke. Frequently his calculations were upset when Patrick did not call or broke yet another date and he would labour through an evening, fighting to regain an equilibrium that was so easily lost. Time and again all that kept Adrian from falling into a black pit of despair was the unalterable belief that one day Patrick would discover his own repressed emotion and Adrian's faithfulness, his dogged love, would be granted its reward.

It was almost seven when Patrick walked into view, an unknown youth in jeans and earrings by his side. Adrian waited for the gestures of farewell but saw with heavy disappointment that both came in.

"Hi," said Patrick cheerfully, standing by the table. "Been waiting long?"

"About an hour," Adrian tried to return the smile.

"You shouldn't have bothered. I'm afraid we can't stay."

"Can't stay?" Adrian smothered but could not control his reaction.

"We're going for dinner. It's Susie's birthday."

The name was a blank, but he might still have been invited. "At least have a coffee." The words struggled out from the midst of pain and confusion.

"A quick one." Patrick signalled to the waitress, sat, made room for the boy beside him. "By the way, this is Nick. Adrian."

"Hi." Nick looked over, young and cute and arrogant.

"Hi." There was no sign of affection between them, yet Adrian knew that they had spent the day and would spend the night together. It was not jealousy he felt, but a lack of worth, a sense of failure as great as the love he felt.

The waitress came, took their order. "So, what have you been doing?" Patrick turned back to ask.

Waiting for you, Adrian wanted to say; thinking about you, wanting you, wanting to talk with you, wanting to kiss you, make love with you. "The same old thing."

"It would just go on." His thoughts interrupted, Adrian looks up to see himself back in the pub, face to face with the man in black. It is more crowded now and others press against them, but the only person that he is aware of is his companion.

"You'd never give up," the man goes on. "You'd think he'd eventually change, but he wouldn't. He doesn't want intensity in a partner; he wants someone who will laugh with him, who won't make any demands, who'll eventually go his own way. You'd be the one to change. You'd grow bitter, unpleasant." " But I love . . ." Adrian stops, aware that Patrick has never existed. "But surely loving him would be better than loving no one at all."

The man shakes his head. "It's love of a sort, but loving a dream is an excuse for not being able to love reality. It's a sign of failure, of fear of yourself, of fear of the world."

"I'm not afraid of the world."

"Aren't you? Most people are, in their way."

"And how am I?"

"How are you afraid? You're afraid of opening yourself to someone who'll make demands of you — even though that is what you want most of all. So you have affairs with young men who have no expectations of you, or whose expectations are nowhere near yours."

The picture, Adrian realises, is true. He tries to collect his thoughts, is dimly conscious of the music and conversations around him. "Anyway, I meant something different. I meant to love and be loved in return."

"By anyone? That's simple." The man's eyes twinkle in amusement.

"By someone like Patrick. Someone physically attractive. Young, good-looking."

"Totally devoted to you?"

"Sure."

"I'm in here."

Adrian closed the front door, walked through to the warmth and smell of cooking in the kitchen.

"Had a good day?" Patrick asked, turning from the stove in anticipation of a kiss.

"Okay. And you?"

"Mm," Patrick nodded, turned back to his task. Adrian took off his jacket, slumped into a chair, looked up at Patrick's cropped hair, his loose black shirt, the tapering waist and shapeless jeans. There was something infinitely attractive about the sight and yet also something infinitely disappointing. "What did you do?"

"Shopped. Cleaned. Watched TV. Here, taste this." Patrick brought over a spoon in which some sauce lay. "Good, isn't it?"

"Yes," Adrian agreed, without paying the flavour much attention. "Did you go job-hunting?"

"I did *not* go job-hunting." Patrick's tone verged on the sarcastic. "I will go job-hunting when I'm ready to. At the moment I'm quite happy living on the dole and with you. Understand?"

"But if . . ."

"If I had a job we would see less of each other. I would be tired, I wouldn't have the time or energy to cook and I certainly wouldn't eat your cooking." He grinned. "I don't need a job, not at the moment. Why do you keep insisting? To stop me living off you?"

"No." As long as enough money was coming in Adrian didn't care who earned it. "I just thought you might be happier out of the house."

"Doing what? Working in a bar? Being a security guard? Filing papers in some office? I did it for five years and now I want a rest. One day maybe I'll go back to college and train for something more 'useful'." He turned down the gas, added water. "If we're both happy, what's the problem?"

Adrian wished he knew. He had thought that no matter how intensely he loved Patrick — and he did — he would love him more if he had a job, a life of his own. But if Adrian were honest with himself he would have to admit that that was not true. Whatever was missing between them would not be found by Patrick working a nine-to-five job. It was a sense of excitement, of mystery, that Adrian had always sought and that Patrick, despite all his devotion, could not provide.

If only there were some way to create that magic. But there was not. He sat watching the only man he had every truly loved chop vegetables and stir saucepans, imagined the scene repeated day after day and felt unaccountably depressed. "No," he said quietly to himself, "this isn't what I wanted."

"No?" the now-familiar voice breaks through. "But it's love. Love returned. You were in love with him, weren't you?"

"Yes," Adrian says, remembering the dream and other fast-fading moments. "But . . ."

"But love isn't everything. Sometimes it isn't even enough."

"It should be, dammit." Adrian's voice rises, but no one around seems to hear him or react. "It is for others. It's all I ever wanted and now you're telling me it won't make me happy."

"I'm not telling you that." The man's voice is quiet, reassuring, kind. "I'm only showing you that what you think you want isn't necessarily what you really want."

"How do you know what I want? I want Patrick, okay? Not the first one and not the second one. A bit of both, somewhere in between; I'm not sure."

"Oh, if you want him, you can have him. He can be anything you want him to be. He's over there."

Adrian turns, sees a young blond sipping at a drink, looking casually round the bar. A kaleidoscope of false and pleasant memories rushes through his mind, making love, talking, on holiday together, holding hands in the cinema. Yet as Patrick's gaze approaches, Adrian quickly turns away, unwilling to be seen.

"Well?" the man asks.

"Let me think." Adrian looks down at the warm beer lying at the bottom of his glass.

"He doesn't have everything you want. No young man does.

Confidence, calmness, wisdom, humour, an ability to surprise, understanding."

"But that's what I want. All that."

"All that is much more than love, no matter how deep or desperate."

"So you can give Steve and Derek what they want but you can't give me what I want."

"But I can."

They look at each other. Suddenly Adrian understands.

"If you only want love, you'll find it with Patrick. It'll be sincere and worthy and — most of the time — you'll be quite happy."

"And if I want more?"

"You know the answer."

Adrian finishes his drink, puts the glass down. Tearing his eyes away from his companion, he looks round. It seems as if the other men in the bar, the bar itself, the furniture, the fruit machines and the music are all somehow faded and dull. Against them, like an actor before a poorly painted backdrop, this man in black with his spreading stomach, his veined hands, his lined face and thinning hair is alive, immediate, real. More than that, he is the unknown, the excitement that Patrick and all the others lack. This isn't what Adrian expected; in all his fantasies he has never dreamt of this. It is, however, what he wants, the thrill and fear of standing on the highest diving-board the moment before launching oneself into space.

"Shall we go?"

Adrian nods, follows his companion, his lover, through the crowd towards the door. As he does so, he passes Patrick. Their eyes meet, Patrick shows interest, but Adrian smiles and walks on.

OBLIVION

I dropped anchor a hundred yards from shore, weary yet reluctant to be near land once more. I do not know how long I had been at sea. Weeks certainly, months perhaps. Sailing slowly round Africa, I had glimpsed the continent from afar but never wanted to approach; there was pain there and I bore too much pain of my own.

I had last docked in an Asian port where the gleaming yachts of the rich turned their backs to the juggernauts of commerce strung out along the opposite shore. My barque with its triple masts and yards of rigging was out of place, a symbol of values and origins that my neighbours could not identify. But, when I wish, I am courteous and for a time I was welcome as quiet host and thoughtful guest. There is, after all, a common language in such places — the grammar of wealth, the vocabulary of currency and commodity, the accents of clothing and custom. But I soon tired of self-absorbed businessmen, their middle-aged wives and uncertain and arrogant children. And so one night, on impulse, I pushed back from the pier, slid out into the sound and hoisted sail in the shadow of a passing tanker.

I chose the small harbour at random. Balking at the English Channel and the memories that lay beyond, I found myself sailing aimlessly through the Irish Sea. On the west coast of Scotland I thought I might find the illusion of tranquility. So I pulled out an old chart and plotted a course past an outcrop where boulders lurked below the surface like animals in the jungle and over a sandbank which was passable at high tide. It was early dawn and the shore lights winked in loneliness as I watched the clatter of the anchor chain. When the sails had been stowed and decks cleared, I looked round the bay at the handful of small boats bobbing with quiet dignity, heard the cack of a seagull and the growl of a distant car and went below to sleep through the day.

In the early evening I rowed across to the beach, hauled the dinghy over the pebbles above the highwater mark and entered the bar that beckoned like a lighthouse. Two men were playing darts; behind the counter a woman in her forties replaced bottles as a tall and dark youth in his early twenties poured me a whisky with a quiet greeting. I thanked him and took the glass to a corner of the room where I sat and watched the evening unfold.

Locals drifted in, nodded at me and greeted each other in accents as thick as my own. It was a small community, indifferent to strangers, and I welcomed the fact that they left me undisturbed. An hour passed before a quiet voice broke through the silence I had drawn around myself and asked if mine was the newly-arrived yacht. My eyes focused on the bartender picking up glasses from the table in front of me and I answered yes, if he meant the triple-master. "It's a lovely boat," he said in the local lilt. "Where are the rest of the crew?" Dead, I almost replied. "I handle her alone." He looked at the tired, aging man before him and smiled, polite and disbelieving. How long was I going to stay? A month, I said, maybe more. Here? he asked. I nodded. But why? For peace and quiet, I said.

At closing time I watched the customers drift away. My drink waited, for I was in no hurry to return to a berth where I might not easily find rest. The young man came over with a beer in his hand. "Do you mind if I join you?" he asked. I shook my head, surprised that he did not want me to leave. "There's no hurry," he reassured me. "The law knows we don't serve after time and mother" — his head tilted towards the woman behind the bar — "lets me clear up in my own time."

There was a silence that neither of us wished to fill. "You're from here?" I asked eventually. "Aye, but I've been away. Came back, like you, for peace and quiet." There was a softness in his voice that suggested vulnerability, yet deeper strength. His eyes were dark and his expression serious. We talked for a little about the village, the nearby farmers and the fishing that had died. There were tourists in summer, English, Americans and Europeans who slept upstairs and filled the bar with their enthusiasm and questions before driving on to Oban or Kyle. He wondered where I came from, where I was going. I answered politely and he let the matter drop. "It's a beautiful boat," he said. "I saw it when I woke. I've never seen one like it before." I asked if he had sailed and he told me of days spent on his father's smack, of weekends on a rich friend's yacht. "I'd love to have my own boat." His longing hung in the air.

At last the room and our glasses were empty, the conversation at an end. At the door I thanked him for his company, stood in the street for a moment letting my eyes adjust to the dark and made my way over the beach to the outline of the dinghy. As I pulled away, I saw his silhouette watching, eventually turn and go indoors. The windows stayed lit for a moment and then only the few streetlamps marked the shore.

An hour later, as I lay in my bunk, the nightmares began. The months at sea had allowed me to forget not their existence but their intensity; once again I lay helplessly buffeted by my past and future, by the women I had known and the woman I had killed, by men who had sailed and died with me, by hurricanes and becalmed seas. In fear of my life, my soul, yet knowing both were long since lost, I sat up and lit the lamp to banish these visions. Yet all I saw as I stared across the cabin were the hundreds who bayed for my life, all I heard were the agonies of the damned and all I could feel were the flames of hell. Against my will again and again I kissed her lips, held her breast, lifted the knife, saw the blood surge, protested my innocence rather than a repentance I did not feel, heard sentence pronounced and set sail to struggle against storms within and without for year after endless year.

The light of dawn brought calm and I slept exhausted through much of the day. A voice hailing woke me and I peered through the porthole to see the young man from the bar balancing in a dinghy a few yards away. In irritation I pulled on clothes and made my way up on deck. On seeing my mood and dishevelled state, he apologised. "I didn't know you were asleep. I just wondered if I you needed any provisions."

"I haven't taken stock," I lied.

"I brought milk and bread and eggs, stuff like that." He gestured at the cardboard box beside him. "I can take back anything you don't need." I did not want the obligation of payment or gratitude, but I have learnt that kindness is better received than refused. So I welcomed him aboard, took the box down to the galley and offered him the hospitality of alcohol or tea. Cups in hand, we sat on deck in the warmth of autumn sunshine, watching the waves and the anchored boats apparently abandoned by their owners, the distant headland with its stubble of grass.

After a time he asked if he might look over the boat. Of course, I said, standing up, glad to play host to an honest guest. I showed him details of the rigging, the stowed sails, where sheets and halyards were coiled. Again he amazed that I could handle her alone, that all was so neat and clean. Below, he peered into my cabin, with its bedclothes strewn across the floor, and the crew's quarters, neat, prim, untouched. The oil stove and the brass taps of the galley he saw as quaint, the sextant and compass as fascinating. "And your stores?" "Here," I said, sliding back a door, and he stared at rows of packets and tins in languages he did not recognise and I had forgotten.

Back on deck, in another lull, I asked where he had been and why he had come back. Glasgow, he said, to help his mother. I sensed the same reticence in his words, the same avoidance of truth, that he no doubt sensed in mine. We talked then of the sea and of the world, but whatever had happened in that city, in his past, had scarred him, for he spoke not with the aspirations of youth but the pessimism of age. Yet his tone was friendly, undemanding and cheerful and in the conversation and silences that accompanied it I heard the echo of a calm and peace that I had not known for many years.

"I have to be going," he said eventually, unwinding the painter that yoked his dinghy. "Are you coming over this evening?" Probably, I said. I watched him row with steady, solid strokes as he had watched me the night before. It was already dusk, the streetlamps were lit and brightness shone at the windows of houses. I think he waved from the pier, but it was too far to see and, suddenly tired, I turned and went below.

That night I sat again in the bar, my neighbour a man like many who have strong opinions and a strong belief that you wish to hear them. His words washed over me, leaving only the residue of his insecurity, the aftermath of emotions that had shrivelled in the furnace of an overactive intellect. My attention wandered, found nothing to cling to. The young man I now saw as a friend smiled but was too busy for more words than welcome. For a time I watched not him but his mother, wondering if it was from her that her son had inherited his patience and politeness. She was a handsome woman, with generous hair that had once been blonde and features complemented by the lines of middle age. But as she moved from counter to bottle to till, listening to one customer while serving another, glancing over the room to see who had arrived and where they stood or sat, she did so with more efficiency than warmth. I looked for, but could not see, kindness in her eyes, affection in her smile.

The other women in the bar were even further from my desire. Two teenage girls with boyfriends sat in tight coloured clothes that missed the mark of fashion; a grandmother, a local character, chaffed all in hearing; wives sat with men in the posture of many years of marriage. There was none that I would want to talk to, none who would want to talk to me. I closed my eyes and thought back over the monotony of the past years, saddened that I no longer knew what kind of woman I wanted, what kind of woman could love me.

When first I set sail I was frantic, seeking out every woman in every port I docked. I turned first to the beautiful for, although in middle age, I still confused physical attraction with perfection, smiles with sympathy, the surrendering of virtue with self-

sacrifice. Yet my predicament did not allow me to ignore women
who were unattractive, women whose youth had given way to
character, women whose dishonesty was as apparent as their
cosmetics. So I wooed each I met with an ardour that at times was
close to violation. Some were flattered, others bewildered, not
a few were hostile. I pursued them regardless, interpreting
against all evidence their every gesture in the light of my own
desperation, defeated only when they fled my company, when
their menfolk challenged me, when the nightmares had become
incessant and drove me back to sea.

Over the years, unwillingly, I came to understand that such
behaviour was selfish and self-defeating, a repetition of my
earlier crime. I tried then another course, turning from pleas of
passion to pleas for sympathy, plainly stating my past and laying
bare my future. A rare few responded with pity, that most
captivating and destructive of emotions, but with most all that
my honesty engendered was laughter at my presumption, dis-
gust at my crime or disbelief at my words. And so each time I
spoke, I would watch my companion carefully, waiting for her
eyes and heart to grant the absolution that would set me free, but
all that I saw, again and again, was the abyss that forever
separated me from the human race.

Eventually I resolved to court no more. For, I realised,
whether I spoke as an ardent lover or a repentant criminal, it was
not my companion I wanted but the peace she represented. No
matter which path I pursued, whether I acknowledged my
situation or disguised it, the rejection was the same. For many
years I despaired of ever finding freedom. But then, I argued,
perhaps my greatest hope lay not in my own persuasion but in
others' altruism. And so I began to treat women with the same
politeness as I addressed their fathers, brothers and husbands.
Some indeed, finding me handsome yet distant, sought me out
and I spent many pleasant hours in their company. Yet when it
seemed that intimacy was at its intensest, when affection had
earned the name of love and the moment had come to tell my
story, I would do so, only to see each, abruptly or on reflection,
withdrawing from my life and leaving me alone with the sea and

my vessel once more.

Although I could never become indifferent to my fate, with the passing of time I began to accept it. I allowed myself a succession of mistresses who saw me as no more than an eccentric but undemanding seafarer and in their company watched the unfolding of history. I saw the seas explode with ships and trade and violence and the wilderness retreat from the aggression of cities and industry. I became distant, omniscient, no longer surprised by any human action, no matter how foolish or cruel. As clearly as through glass, I could glimpse through one person's boast or another's demurral, through a lover's promise or a child's plea, the brutal fears and desires that lay at the heart of individual lives. Yet if I turned my glance upon myself, my vision failed; there was no clarity, only a heavy, dark blur of emotions that I could never identify.

For a week I did not return to the bar, preferring the memory of its company to the company itself. I stayed on board, cleaning, doing unnecessary repairs, reading and writing. Twice I rowed to the headland and tied the dinghy to a rock on which other boats would have quickly broken, before climbing to the peak to survey the coast and distant hills. There was a calmness there that I welcomed, a sense of age and peace; apart from the streetlamps in the village and the grey tarmac that threaded across the landscape, I reckoned the bay had looked little different when I was young.

My young friend rowed out one day, concerned at my absence and the thought that I might be unwell. We talked a little as I thanked him for his solicitude and ignored the opportunity to invite him aboard. Disappointed but not offended, he smiled as he rowed back and I wondered for a moment whether the disruption would have been more welcome than the solitude. Eventually, however, I ran out of petty tasks, found my mind with nothing to distract it from fear of the nightmares ahead. And so after dark one evening, as a westerly rocked the boat and worried the sea, I wrapped myself in woollens and waterproofs and made for the shore. The bar was half-full, the young man, working alone, greeted me, and, with the whisky I had come to enjoy, I settled in a seat by the window.

It was towards the end of the evening that I noticed the tension between my friend, clearing a table, and two young men of similar age sitting with their girlfriends nearby. There were words I only half-heard and a sudden movement which made him spill the contents of a glass. As he reached over to wipe the beer away, the comment "Keep your hands off me!" pierced and silenced the conversations around.

"I've no intention of touching you," my friend said in quiet tones.

"That wasn't the case a couple of years ago. In fact," the youth stood up, "I've never given you the reply you deserved."

The fist was ready to strike and no one was prepared to protest. I did not doubt that my friend could defend himself, but before I could think I found myself shouting "Sit down, sir, and behave yourself!"

The shock of the authority in my voice caused the aggressor to hesitate while the surprise from the rest of the crowd dissolved some of the tension. "Who the hell are you?" he asked uncertainly.

"It doesn't matter," I replied, "but I see no point in fighting."

My friend, carefully, moved away.

"But you don't know what he did." There was a disagreeable whine in the voice.

"No," I admitted, "but it obviously wasn't murder."

"Probably nothing he didn't want," a voice came from the crowd. Suddenly there was laughter, of both amusement and derision. Not quite understanding, but aware that the danger had passed, I sat back in my chair. The stranger sat down, red-faced, and started talking to his companions in words I could not hear. My friend took dirty glasses to the bar, served the next customer. The old woman beside me shook her head and I learnt that the aggressive young man was known for getting drunk.

It was only when the bar closed that its caretaker was free to come over. "Thanks," he said. I shrugged my shoulders; "I didn't do anything."

"You made things easier for me."

I noticed his tension, but could not tell whether it was from fear or rage. "Are you all right?" I asked.

He nodded. "More or less, but I've been expecting something like this."

"What do you mean?"

"It's a private matter." My expression must have said something, for he added, "but if you want to know . . ."

I was curious, but did not wish to listen in the anonymity of the bar. So I suggested he lock up and we row over to the yacht, where a quarter of an hour later we sat in the warmth of the cabin, rocked gently by a night breeze. In comfort and privacy and encouraged by alcohol he relaxed and began to talk about himself.

He had lived all his life in this part of the world, moving to the village from the nearby town when his father had bought the bar a few months before he died. He had not been unhappy, but in his teens a desire for companionship had grown too strong to be satisfied by the few other youths he knew. So one day he had gone to Glasgow, staying first with an aunt and then with friends he made in the city. He had looked for and found work, but had sought with greater eagerness the friendship that he desired. At last he met a man ten years older than himself, an architect, a traveller, someone with wit and wisdom. They had lived together for two years when the older man fell ill, a lingering, wasting illness from which he died. So my friend, burdened by an anger and sadness that he could not resolve, had returned home because there was nowhere else, he said, that he wanted to be.

"But the boy who wanted to fight you," I asked, "how does he fit in?"

He looked at me as if astonished by my naivety. "Years ago I wanted to make love with him."

For a moment the words did not make sense; when they did, it threw the story of his friend in Glasgow into another and truer perspective. We stared at each other in silence. I had an image of his body naked against another man's; the idea was repugnant and I pushed it away.

I knew that there were men with these desires, had known them in my crew. But I had always seen their actions as impelled by drunkenness, perversion, the absence of women, acts which reflected the instincts of animals, not the tenderness which men and women share.

"I thought you understood," he said, seeing my hesitation.

"You were in love with this man?" I asked. "As I . . ." have never loved, "As I might love a woman?"

"Yes, I loved him."

"But a woman . . ." The words died. I realised to my surprise that his expression, his tone, had suggested a more honest and therefore deeper love than in all my years I had ever achieved. "But men and women are so different." My words were weak, said nothing of what I intended, and as I heard them I realised how irrelevant they were.

He smiled. There was another silence. I stared across the table and saw a man much older and wiser than he appeared. Floundering between distaste and lack of understanding, I held back words that would only reveal my ignorance. Reaching for the bottle, I filled my glass, offered him more but he refused.

"I've told you my past," he said. "Now it's your turn."

I pretended not to understand.

"What aren't you telling me?"

I could neither lie nor tell the truth. "Many things," I said.

"This boat," he said. "The crew. Where you came from. None of what you've told me makes sense."

I closed my eyes, naked, exhausted, afraid.

"Just how old are you?" he asked.

I looked at him. "Old. Much older than you think."

"How old?" he repeated.

I told him.

He sat silent for a minute, then shook his head. "I don't want to believe you. But I do." He looked down at the empty glass in his hand, finally glanced up. "Tell me about it."

I did not want to, afraid that he would understand too little or too much. Nor had I ever told my story to another man. But his stare was a plea for honesty that I could not refuse and behind that lay the promise of a temporary catharsis. So, slowly, and with none of the anxiety and flattery that had accompanied the tale each of the hundreds of times when I told it to a woman, I took him back to my house in Amsterdam, to my wife, my crime and my doom. I spoke slowly, listening to my words before I uttered them, offering only facts and rejecting rationale and justification. He asked no questions, listened with no other expression than sympathy, so that at times I wondered whether he had heard or understood.

"All these years," was his only comment.

"All these years."

I felt drained. There was another long silence into which I sank in gratitude.

"Do you . . ." he eventually said.

I held up a hand. "Don't ask. There's nothing more to say." And although I wanted the subject never to be mentioned again, I knew that that was impossible, that it would always be between us.

The silence returned. Eventually I suggested that we go up on deck to look at the stars. Caressed by the wind, he stared up at the Plough. I silently greeted Orion, wondered whose ships sailed around him. Bringing my gaze down, I saw the string of streetlamps waiting for dawn, heard the lapping of the waves marking the passage of eternity.

He wanted to speak, but did not know what to say. "I have to go," he said at last. "Will you row me back to shore?"

I wanted him to neither go nor stay. "Keep the dinghy," I said. "You can come for me tomorrow. I'm not going anywhere."

He looked up as I threw the painter down at him. "Thank you," he said, "for everything." I watched his silhouette until it merged into the darkness and went below to sit in the empty cabin.

For a week it seemed that the nightmares abated, reverted to no more than unpleasant dreams. I spent more time ashore, not only in the evenings, sitting in the bar, but during the day, exploring the countryside around. Twice my young friend borrowed his mother's car, driving me past compact woods and stark mountains, nervous sheep and sullen cows. We visited the town where he had grown up, and the sight of crowded pavements and illuminated shops, of parents and children, of couples young and old, so moved me that I had to stand aside, to calm my breath and hold back my tears.

In the bar I had become familiar and others became familiar to me. It was a quiet community, similar to many where those who were energetic left and most of those who remained were content with their lives. They saw me as others have often seen me, a man with money but no direction, politeness but little charm. Thus I found I was left alone by those I did not wish to speak to and only spoken to by those who had something to say.

My friend spent more time on the boat and I welcomed his company. Twice we sailed out into the sound and I let him set the sail and take the wheel. He had the ease of experience, eye forever wandering from the top of the mast to the compass to the bow, a light touch on the helm that kept us tightly to our course. It was then that I saw him smile, not only the mouth, but the dark blue eyes which broadened and shone.

We talked often, sometimes about the most trivial of subjects, the weather or the best way of cooking eggs, more rarely about our past and the paths that had brought us here. He had a tact which some never achieve and which in others only comes with maturity but which in him was innate. His questions were quiet and delicate; the answers I gave revealed more of myself than he understood. In return he talked of his short life and the man he had loved. I listened, as if to a symphony from which some harmony was missing, trying to bring together the deep emotion he described with the image, brutish and coarse, of the two of them naked together. And when I heard the description of the man's death, a thin body unable to breathe sinking into extinction, I mourned not for the corpse but the young man he had left behind.

One night a new vision shocked me from the sleep I had come to enjoy. In the court where I had been condemned I watched my friend accused of my crime. As sentence was pronounced he stared into my eyes, wondering why I would not speak. Awake, helpless in my bunk, I followed the crowd that hounded him to my ship, saw him stand helplessly, rigidly, on deck as my crew cast off, watched the vessel sink into the night, his eyes never leaving me for as long as they could see. The scene repeated itself again and again, sometimes with the skeletal figure of his friend pronouncing judgement, sometimes with my wife laughing at me from the crowd. And each time I was caught between the horror of his fate and the horror of my silence.

Dawn brought peace and a few hours of rest. I was woken by his arrival, clambering on board without the permission he no longer needed. He looked down from the deck and saw my expression, the books and belongings that I had tumbled to the floor. "I'm sorry," he said, "do you want me to go?"

I remembered I had offered to take the boat out again that day. "No," I shook my head. "I'm all right."

He waited until I had dressed and recomposed myself and joined him above. It was a perfect day for sailing — blue sky against which a steady wind drove clouds across sea and land. He stowed the bag he had brought and the box of fresh provisions, brewed coffee and came back on deck. Towing the dinghy, we tacked south out of the bay, then headed towards the islands that lay on the horizon. He stood at the helm as I sat out of the breeze in the cockpit. Standing tall, with the wind ruffling his hair, he resembled one of the heroic mariners of fiction rather than the squat, disfigured men with whom I had always sailed.

"I could do this forever," he said.

I did not appreciate the remark.

His look almost made me apologise. "I was serious," he said.

"Then you don't know what you mean."

"Yes, I do." He fell silent as he corrected our course. "I mean not going back. I mean taking this boat and sailing it out into the Atlantic as far as it will go. I mean being your crew for the rest of my life."

For a moment it seemed as if the vision of the previous night was continuing, but no, this was a reality that I could to a small extent influence.

"You still don't know what you mean."

"I do," and there was a strength in his voice that was new to me. "You're the one that doesn't understand. I want you." His eyes fell from the horizon to hold mine and there was such intensity there that I thought I saw his soul reflected. "I want you," he repeated.

"For what?" I asked, suddenly disturbed and angry. "For whatever you did in that man's bed?"

"Yes," he said quietly, his eyes once again on his task. "But that's not important. I just want to be with you. Always."

"Why?"

"Because I'm in love with you."

The word was strange, one which I only sometimes understood and which formed no link between him and me.

"There's nothing for me at home. You've seen that. And I don't want to go back to Glasgow or London or any other city. They're just big and concrete and noise. People don't have time to be themselves." We were in deeper waters now and the boat dove and rose; his hands on the wheel adjusted the course automatically, without thinking. "I just want to be on my own somewhere, with someone like you."

"Someone like me?" Anger broke the amazement that had kept me silent. "There is no one like me. You haven't heard what I said. You don't know what it means to sail with me. You would never, ever, come back."

"I'm sorry," he said. "With you. And I know I would never come back. I don't want to come back. In the bag I brought with me is everything I need. Clothes, books, money. We need never return."

I thought of taking the wheel, but to sail back to the bay was against the wind and if he was not willing, it would be a fruitless struggle like many I had had before.

"Why condemn yourself?" I said eventually. "You're young. There must be many of your kind who would like you, and who you would like. Why not try to find one and lead a normal life?"

"Throw away a gold coin in case I find a silver one — is that what you're asking me? And what is a 'normal life'? A house, a job, someone quiet and safe? A normal life is the one I choose to lead. And I want to lead it with you."

"You don't know me!" my anger returned. "You see only the politeness, you don't see the hate." I stared at him with a sudden loathing for the humanity he represented, a loathing that emerged after festering for years. "I would kill you this instant if I thought it would bring me peace. I would fire a rifle into your brain. I would take a sword and pierce your heart. I would tie you to a rack and hack off your arms and legs one by one, leaving you to bleed to death if it would bring me what I sought. Don't you understand that you mean nothing to me, that my own peace is all that I want?"

He said nothing. I could not read his expression. I startled to see that my words had come true: his torso was skewered to an invisible wall, the stumps of arms and legs dripping blood as he looked at me in love and compassion. I closed my eyes and he was still there; I screamed "Forgive me!" and fell to the deck, where I lay for hours or seconds gripped by his pain before I looked up and saw him standing calmly, hands on the wheel, eyes out to sea.

He made no comment as I slowly gathered myself up against the pitching of the sea. Eventually my shaking ceased, my breath slowed, my mind returned; I sat up and straightened my clothes. I expected him to speak, to offer some platitude, but he said nothing. I realised that I had never given way like this in front of another before. Each night that I faced the nightmares it was always alone. If others approached, the visions would fade and somehow I could recompose myself. I did not know why the same had not happened with him.

He glanced down at me, his expression unchanged, before looking back at the sea. "What are you thinking?" I asked, challenged by his calm. "That here is a senile old man who tells absurd tales and has nervous breakdowns?"

He shook his head. "I don't know what I'm thinking. There are no words. But I feel . . ."

"Pity?"

"I don't know. I don't think so. Admiration, perhaps."

"Admiration?" I scorned. "For what? A lunatic? A murderer? A ghost?"

"For what you've been through. For what you are, a man who . . ."

He did not fill the silence. "Who what?" I asked.

"Don't ask me; I can't explain. I only know that I love you."

A coldness swept over me, a coldness as frightening as the peal of thunder and as welcome as a shower of rain. I did not want to hear any more, I did not want to say any more, I wanted only to close my eyes and lie motionless until the world had come to an end.

I looked forward and saw we were not far from our destination. The island had a bay, he had said, where we could anchor, ruins of a castle he had once explored. I stood up, walked round the deck checking winches and ropes, looked back at the dinghy bobbing unwillingly behind us. "A drink?" I offered, going below. He asked for coffee and I brought it up with some biscuits he had provided. I took the helm and he sat in my place, back to the wind, feet on the opposite bench. He seemed so much more mature than his age — a man in charge of his life rather than a boy at the mercy of others.

The silence deepened, and when he broke it, it was almost as if I had known what he was going to say.

"What do I do?" he asked.

I pretended not to understand.

"If you won't take me with you, what do I do to set you free? Do I cut my throat? Tie rocks to my legs and jump into the ocean? Ask you for a gun so that I might shoot myself?"

"Don't talk about it," I said.

"Do we die together?"

"Don't use that word!" I shouted. "Never, ever, use that word again!"

He looked away, watched a seagull in the wind. "Don't you see," he said at last, "that I can't let you go?"

"Of course you can." My voice was quiet again. "In time you'll find someone."

"Now you don't understand," he said, in tones of anger and regret. "You don't even try to understand. I don't want 'someone'. I don't want to spend my life looking for something I've already found. And if I can't be with you in life I want to be with you in death."

I did not need to watch my course to know that we would follow it. But I could not look at him at that moment. My heart, my soul, was filled with an emotion I had never known, a joy, a hope, a love and a sadness at hearing the words I had waited for centuries to hear. In that moment I had a vision of the two of us together sailing across the world in a friendship based on a peace I had never known. We would grow old together and I would find the happiness I had never found in my wife or in the hundreds of women I had known over the years. We would share everything, meals, sunrises, storms, ideas; even, I realised without apprehension, a bed.

And if that vision were not enough, there was another which was even stronger. The two of us in the eye of a hurricane, a few minutes' calm before the wind returned. A hundred yards away the shoals of some shore. The gale ripping the sails, driving the vessel towards the rocks, breaking its back and throwing us to the waves. And the sweet, sweet sensation of being sucked under, lungs filling with water and darkness falling as I saw through the murkiness my companion dying beside me.

My mind returned to the present; we were close to the shore. I looked down at him. Without my asking, without my even seeking, he was indeed offering all that I ever longed for. If he offered once more, I did not know what I would say.

"Well?" he asked.

"Well what?"

"Will you take me?"

I hesitated, then my mind was decided. "If you really want me to," I said, seeing his longing and fear, "I will. But first there is something I can do for you." He did not understand. "The castle," I explained. "You wanted to see it. Something to do with your childhood."

A smile appeared. "There's no need."

"But I want to."

We dropped anchor in shallow waters twenty yards from shore. "Take some food if we need it," I said, as I brought down the sail. He went below and returned with a rucksack of drink and biscuits.

"I'm going down to change my shoes." When I came back up he was waiting in the dinghy. "Catch," I said, throwing him his bag. The movement caught him off-balance, the dinghy flailed and spun. I threw off the painter, rushed forward and with more thought than effort, hauled up the sail, watched the anchor rise from the seabed. In that second the wind changed direction, swept the boat round towards the headland and out to sea. I made my way back to the wheel, eyes focussed on nothing as I blotted out the cries behind me. He called my name, begged me to stop, I heard the desperate splash of oars as he tried to pursue me, the cries of pain fading as I headed out to sea. My eyes were dry as they clung to the horizon, but my heart wept for the only person who had loved me and offered me oblivion.

AN
ODD FELLOW

We were not so lost that we could not have retraced our steps, but we had little idea of where we were going. Behind us was the Avenida Rio Branco, the commercial heart of Rio, which at night was merely a ribbon of light along which growled impatient buses and taxis; ahead lay dark and silent streets that we had no real wish to explore. Tired, untidy figures walked by, staring at us with an expression I hoped was no more than curiosity. More than once I was startled to see the hunched bodies of drunks, children, a whole family, sleeping in shop doorways.

At any other time we would have had the sense to be nervous, to turn back and find a taxi that would take us to our hotel and the lights and crowds of Copacabana. But the argument which had finally broken out over our evening meal still kept us apart, leaving Brian set between sulking and anger and myself more resigned than repentant. By morning the temper would subside to the occasional sardonic remark as we packed, and the long flight home would lever us back into reality, but at that moment our separate prides were leading us further into an unknown, perhaps dangerous, part of the city.

The direction we had taken brought us to a square where men, buses and a row of yellow taxis loitered as if waiting for some sergeant-major to come and shout and bully them into order. It was as dark as the streets we had just walked through — I could make out trees and benches and wondered if I saw the silhouette of a dried-up fountain — but snack-bars on its perimeter threw a light towards us that was less inviting than reassuring.

"I want a drink," Brian announced, suddenly leaving the pavement and crossing over to the nearest bar. I followed and let him order two beers, aware that once again the heat and humidity had drained from my body the sweat that now hung heavy in my trousers and shirt. Refreshed, I leant back against the counter and looked around me. On the other side of the street a taxi had stopped to pick up a fare, two youths passed, their effeminacy exaggerated by the animation of their Portuguese, out of the darkness I heard a shout of anger or exasperation. There were other customers beside us — an unshaven middle-aged man in shorts and a faded T-shirt drinking alone and staring at the scribbled menu on the wall, two older men talking quietly and intently and a woman in her thirties slumped, eyes closed, against the wall, an old and empty handbag hanging from her wrist like a defiant claim to respectability.

"I feel somewhat out of place," I said to Brian, who responded with a shrug that indicated he was not yet in the mood for conversation. Indeed, everything about us, from our sunburnt fair skin to our too-formal clothes, from our ignorance of the language to the fact we had recently shaved, marked us as intruders, sightseers, visitors to the zoo who had somehow entered the monkeys' cage and discovered they were both intelligent and hostile. It was not a comfortable feeling and I suddenly longed to be at home, where I was not a stranger but part of the crowd, where I understood and was myself understood.

A voice dragged me back to reality. The woman who had been leaning against the wall was now standing drunkenly in front of us, repeating some question half-aggressively and half in curiosity. She was dark, negro and, I saw with surprise, not a woman but a man. The lipstick, cheap blouse and feminine slacks could not disguise the roughness of her features, the strength of her arms, the size of her hands; those were no more than symbols of the womanhood she could only aspire to and never attain.

"Don't worry; she's only asking where you come from."

I looked round; it was the solitary drinker on our left who had spoken. He said something to the woman, who grunted, satisfied, and ambled away.

"You're English?" I asked. Beside me, Brian had come out of his mood enough to straighten up and pay attention to our new acquaintance.

"I was born there, but I've lived here for the last ten years. You're here on holiday, I presume." The accent had once been educated British but had fallen into an anonymity that might have been anything from Canadian to Australian.

"Doesn't it look it?"

He smiled and brought his glass over to where we stood. "Mind if I join you? The name's Jack Edwards." We introduced ourselves. "Well, what do you think of our wonderful city?"

Brian shrugged. "It's okay."

"Have you been here long?"

"A fortnight. We're leaving tomorrow."

"What do you think of the local fauna — the girls? Or the boys?" There was not the leer that would have accompanied the question in England. Instead his tone was that of asking about the weather.

"Ask my lover here," Brian suggested bitterly.

"I see." A look of understanding came over Edwards' face. "Don't be too harsh with him. Temptation is not meant to be resisted."

I said nothing, knowing how Brian hated to discuss our private life in public.

"You obviously enjoy it," Brian said.

"I do indeed." Edwards had missed or ignored the sarcasm. "For this taste of paradise I sold my soul many years ago. To a beautiful fallen angel. His name was João — my name, the name of all men — and he was dark and handsome, strong and evil."

"What happened?" I asked.

"I met him one night not far from here and took him back to my apartment. We made love and, as a punishment or a reward for my audacity, he stole my money and my passport and my ticket back to London and when I protested, he punched my stomach so hard that I vomited and held a knife to my face threating to cut open my eye."

"Some angel," Brian commented,

"But he was, he was. You don't know how beautiful he was, how passionate, in love and anger, how perfect he was. He stole everything, not like the common thieves here who apologise when they take your money, who dust you down and hand back your credit cards and hope you have your documents. He was evil, pure evil, and would happily have killed me if I had resisted and given him the excuse."

"Did they catch him?" I asked.

"Who? The police? I never went. They would either have arrested me or ignored me and if they came over would have walked off with anything I had left. They certainly wouldn't have got me my papers back. And so it seemed to me after he had gone and I lay back and the nausea died away, that it was some kind of solution. I had been in Brazil for two years and had to leave because my contract had come to an end. I didn't want to go — I'd fallen in love with this country, with this city — and suddenly I couldn't, because João had taken everything. Oh, I could have gone to the Federal Police to explain the situation and gone to the airline to tell them my ticket had been stolen and to the Consulate to ask for a new passport and be repatriated if necessary and the end result would have been the same. I would have landed in London, that cold and grey city, jobless and owing money and having lost touch with most of the people I had known before I left. I stood at the window and felt the heat and listened to the life in the streets and decided that if I was to be homeless it was preferable to be in Rio, and so I stayed."

In the silence that followed I drank, thirsty again, and poured what was left in the bottle into my glass. Brian did likewise while Edwards waited for us to speak, to criticise or condone. Now that he was standing by me, I saw that he was quite short and overweight. Although his eyes were alive, the deep lines in the suntanned skin that surrounded them suggested tiredness and lack of sleep.

"Has it been worth it?" I asked. "Has this fallen angel granted you everything your heart desires?"

"Not riches," Edwards smiled. "Oh, I can be better dressed than this. I have a pair of trousers and a shirt and even a tie so that when an old friend feels guilty and invites me to dinner I won't let him down. No, I have no wealth, but in its place I have gained what you might call sex but I call love, romance, passion, life at its most urgent and intense."

I did not need to turn to be aware of Brian's near-contempt. Out of the corner of my eye I saw the transvestite who had approached us earlier asking the barman for something which he was refusing. A bus revved in the square and the night seemed even more humid.

"Haven't you seen them?" Edwards broke the silence in a tone that hovered between desperation and enthusiasm. "The boys, the men, the youths? Haven't you seen them on the beaches, lying on the sand, walking by, exercising and straining on the bars? Haven't you seen the strength in their arms, the muscles on their chests, the firm stomachs, the rhythmic movement of their backsides and thighs? They're so proud and aware of themselves, the way they stand, the way they move, gracefully, sensually. Even when they have nothing, they have that. Haven't you gone for a walk and suddenly your belly is taut and your mouth is dry and your eyes are staring at some vision of near-naked masculinity that you thought only existed in your dreams? And you stop and stare and he passes and if he notices you he is either embarrassed but pleased or he smiles and you walk on and there coming towards you is another and then another and you want to take them and make love with all of them." He paused, drank and looked back at me. "You understand, don't you?"

"Well, the boys here are certainly attractive," I said weakly. To say more would have given Brian the excuse to be angry again, to repeat the accusations of raw lechery and infidelity.

"*I* don't understand," said Brian. "You've thrown away ten years of your life for sex?"

"It isn't only the sex," Edwards spoke more calmly, "although that is the essence, the base on which everything else stands. "Each boy is different. Some come from middle-class families

with maids and a car and holidays in Miami, while others live in
the shanty-towns and left school before they were ten so they
could beg or steal or work to support the rest of the family.
They're the ones who are interesting, they're the ones who say
nothing because they're afraid of being laughed at or who talk
and talk, giving out wild, crazy ideas which mean nothing until
you stop and listen and realise how wonderful they are. They're
sixteen, eighteen, twenty; old enough to understand the world
and young enough to have ambition. Then I come along and
they make love with me because this is Rio and they are always
randy and they love to be admired. We talk and if we like each
other we stay together until one or other loses interest and then
I find another and it all starts over again."

He reached for his glass and on emptying it ordered another
beer. I made a clumsy effort, which Edwards interpreted, to ask
for two more and insisted on paying for all three.

"Are they all wonderful?" Brian asked when thirst had been
postponed for another few minutes. I wanted to take off my shirt
but was too European to do so; I tried to stand still, for any
movement brought on another outburst of sweat.

"Yes, in their way," Edwards smiled again, more in apology
than amusement. "No, some lie and steal and hurt. They can be
selfish bastards who offer themselves freely and when you have
made love begin demanding presents or money. Others are
simply thoughtless; they arrange to meet you and then don't
turn up, bring a friend when you want to be alone. But on the
whole . . ."

We drank. Edwards pulled out a packet of cigarettes and lit
one. Brian had relaxed, our argument forgotten, while I was fascinated by this view of the city we had barely got to know. Little
scenes came back to mind, suddenly different, full of meaning,
charged with eroticism where there had only been curiosity or
indifference. Our two weeks in Rio now seemed a waste of time,
like watching a foreign film where the subtitles only came on at
the end.

"How do you live?" Brian asked.

"Money, you mean? Little jobs here and there. I survive and

hurt no one in the process. I don't steal and I don't sell drugs."

His tone was final and Brian, unusually, did not press the point.

"What we've missed," I said half to myself and not sure whether I meant we or I.

"Dawn on Copacabana Beach," said Edwards, "with your arm round a boy who gives all of himself to you because that's all he has in the world. Listening to the waves and seagulls, watching the sky change colour, seeing other couples here and there sharing the same intimacy and warmth. Dressing up at Carnival like a fat maiden aunt greeting and kissing every handsome man you see. Sitting in a bar like this and watching Edson" — he gestured at the transvestite, once again leaning against the wall — "wondering if he'll ever be happy. Sometimes not knowing where your next meal is coming from. Watching a lover sleep, naked because it's too hot for bedclothes. Seeing him leave and knowing there will be another, handsome in a different way and perhaps more demanding, but still willing to make love if the time and circumstances are right. It's paradise — maybe not yours, but it's my paradise." Again he gave us his apologetic smile, but this time it was more relaxed and content.

"But not eternity. How will it end?" It was always Brian who brought conversations back to mundanity.

Edwards shrugged. "It's ending already. The dreaded disease is killing so many. But for me Mephistopheles will return one day. Soon, I expect. One day I'll be stopped by the police and asked for my documents and when they discover I don't have any I'll be arrested. Maybe I'll go to jail, maybe I'll be deported. They'll rough me up, but not a lot, because even though I'm a tramp I'm still a foreigner. But however it happens, you know what? I'm sure João will be there. Maybe he'll be the one to arrest me, but he'll probably be the sergeant, the one who beats me up. He has to be there — it's only fitting."

"And afterwards?" I wondered.

"Afterwards?" He did not seem to understand. "There is nothing afterwards. Whether it's jail or England, it's still limbo. Or rather hell, one crowded, dirty and violent, the other lifeless and cold."

There was a voice behind me. I turned. The barman was making a gesture I could not understand.

"They're closing," Edwards explained. "Time to go home. Where are you staying?" He suddenly seemed very English, the host fetching coats at the end of a dinner party.

"Copacabana. The Trocadero Hotel."

"Well, let's find you a taxi." He finished his beer while Brian and I drank as much of ours as we could, then followed him across the road to the taxi-rank.

"Can we give you a lift?" I offered.

"No, thanks. I don't live far and I'm not sure if I'm going home. I'll just drop a word in the driver's ear so that he doesn't try to cheat you."

I wanted his address, to give him ours, but realised he would refuse. He stood holding the door for us to get into the car, a singular figure, both wise and vulnerable.

"Have a good flight," he said.

We thanked him for his company and wished him well, then the taxi pulled away and the square was behind us and gone.

"An odd fellow," was Brian's only comment, but for several days afterwards, even back in England, he treated me warily, as if suspecting I had caught some strange disease.

FOR THE FIRST TIME IN YOUR LIFE, ANDREW,

you're unhappy. You've never understood the word, have you? It's been what you say you feel when someone at a board meeting puts forward a proposal that is too naive or outrageous to take seriously. It's how you react on Budget Day when the Chancellor unexpectedly robs both Peter and Paul. It's what you told your friends you felt when you discovered an ornament missing or money stolen from your wallet and you knew perfectly well who had taken it. You realise now that you were wrong, that what you were expressing was no more than frustration, irritation or the first stirrings of revenge; never before have you been aware of an emotion such as this, as strong and vague as a headache, never before have you been aware of this pressure behind the eyes, this dryness in the mouth and tautness in the jaw. Never before have you felt so helpless, so lost, so out of control, as if you were in the office and all the laws of economics failed, the market obeyed neither rumour nor reason and you watched all the firm's money, all your efforts, twenty years of work and experience crash to the ground.

And because you have never known the emotion you have not recognised it in others. The boys who lay sprawled across your bed like shipwrecked sailors, exhausted, buffeted by the winds of life, they were unhappy and told you so. You nodded and half-listened to their tales as you fed and housed them, clothed and looked after them, but beyond the simple facts of where they had been and what they had done you neither heard nor understood what they were saying. Luckily, it seldom mattered; what you offered was much more than they had expected and what you received was no more than you wanted.

They were young, these boys, in their late teens or early twenties, come to London in search of whatever they could not find at home — money, affection, security, a career — and were, when you found them, in danger of being pulled under, of drowning in the turbulence of a city where something — the language, the prices, the indifference of others or their own self-confidence — was beyond their capabilities or understanding. You had a talent for picking them out, for spotting in bars and streets those who were lost and downhearted, from among the ordinary bored youths and amateur hustlers who appeared no different to a less experienced eye. You took them home and let them live with you for a few weeks — months if one was not only willing in bed but consciously or instinctively reacted with the right combination of self-assurance and deference, ready to challenge you in humour while always ceding to your familiar frown. They neither expected nor offered much, or rather they offered as they received, hardly aware that the enthusiasm with which they made love was directly proportional to whatever gift you had last handed them and inversely proportional to the length of time they had lived with you. Eventually they left you or you gently eased them out, pushing them back into the life you had rescued them from, into the life they no longer feared, waving them goodbye and forgetting them as soon as your door was closed, as soon as the next drifting youth came into view. It was no more than they expected; most looked on you kindly, were grateful for what you had done, but were relieved to withdraw from a presence that had become embarrassing or overbearing, to withdraw from your age or your essential coldness, from a lifestyle that for some was too pleasant or too claustrophobic to accept. It was only in later years that they looked back on you with more fondness than regret, seeing you then for what you were, a stage for them, a necessary transition rather than a goal.

But you never realised how unhappy some of these boys had once been. If they lost that emotion, if their feelings calmed and they began to look upon life with more optimism, it was only because you offered them time and comfort to recover, to prepare, to grow older and wiser, to start again. You did nothing to help them because you were not aware they needed help. It never occurred to you either that one could suffer in any way but physically or even, occasionally, that the cause of suffering could be you. Yet amongst several there was one boy you particularly remember, unwillingly, who did not merely accept your hospitality in return for his body, who was not only happy to keep house for you, to cook and clean and entertain, but who saw in you a man that was strong and intelligent, ambitious and successful, a man that had taste and style and enough concern to have picked him and looked after him. It was only natural to him to respond, to give you whatever he could. There was, in short, a boy who fell deeply in love with you.

He was nineteen, twenty, different from the rest in that he had a home, an expensive bedsit in greyest Streatham, and a job, as a clerk in the office of an engineering firm. Nevertheless, when you saw him in that bar in Soho you recognised him as a boy who would respond to you, who would slip into your long-established routine. So he gave up his job, grateful not to have to spend his day surrounded by middle-aged draughtsmen and teenage girls who gossiped about him, and left his room with its view of a brick wall inset with a solitary hostile window and moved into your small but so very comfortable house in Chelsea.

Of course he loved to be there, to be able to lie in each morning, to look forward to leisurely afternoons and evenings out, at a musical, having dinner or simply drinking in the pub next door. Of course he was charmed by a lifestyle where money seemed to come so effortlessly it was unimportant, where everyone he met was good-looking or intelligent or influential, where life itself was easier than he had ever imagined it to be. It was easy for you to recognise the signs in him that you had recognised so often before — the quick intake of breath, the new and sudden enthusiasms, the poorly concealed and not always temporary greed — and you smiled to yourself, pleased to have brought about, to be able to control, these reactions as carefully and subtly as the responses under fingers and mouth in the privacy of your bed.

What you never understood, or rather what you could not accept, was that with this boy the emotion went deeper, that much as he loved the luxury he loved you more. He saw what the others could not or did not want to see — the loneliness that you hid and protected from yourself and the world. You were not aware of it, but he was, perhaps because he himself was lonely and saw in you his reflection. He didn't see deeply, he didn't understand much, he only knew that he was happy with you, that he could put up with your occasional pettiness and flashes of anger, that he could even accept you did not feel as strongly for him as he did for you. In time, he believed, you would grow not only to accept his presence but to want him to be there, you would understand that he was not like the others who had used you in the same way you had used them, you would, eventually, fall in love with him.

He was wrong. He saw himself getting closer to you, saw you trusting him more and more, but he did not realise that the process was not inevitable, that one day you would react, you would wake up to what you saw as a threat, an intimacy and a familiarity that you did not want. It was the most frightening and saddest day of his life to hear you say one morning, coldly, calmly, as if you were at the office instructing an underling to perform a routine task, that he had to leave that day, that here was a cheque to tide him over the next few weeks. Odd, isn't it, that when you saw he had cashed the cheque you were relieved, glad to have confirmed that all he had ever wanted from you was money, that his increasing affection only masked his subtle greed. It never occurred to you that he took the money out of desperation, that for days after he left he lived more roughly than most of the others you ever picked up, that while he was wandering the streets or getting drunk he was not sure whether his next step was to kill himself or find a job. All you knew was that it had been, for reasons you did not understand, increasingly uncomfortable to live with him and that you did no more than what you had told and would tell many others to do.

Oh, he survived, came through that crisis and now lives quietly and happily in the suburbs with a lover who, perhaps not surprisingly, resembles you in some ways, provides not only the financial but the emotional security you could never offer. If he were to meet you, it would be awkward for him, but not unpleasant, perhaps more upsetting for you now that you understand all that he went through. Strange, isn't it, that in your mid-forties, at the height of a successful City career, surrounded by the comforts that have always been your right, with the respect and companionship of the appropriate friends, life apparently fully under control, you should be attacked by this new and unaccountable pain?

You're not stupid, of course. You know its cause. What alarms you is that you have no idea what to do about it, whether to ignore it or fight it or soothe it away. You might even give it a name but are afraid to do so, afraid that to call it love or obsession or infatuation is tantamount to admitting weakness or failure, tantamount to admitting that you are no more than a teenager, no better than one of your boys talking about their first dreamy affairs. So in place of a definition, a description, a confession, there lies in your mind only his picture, his oval face with its short, spiky and impossibly fair hair, his blue eyes and the garish earrings, his cocky expression, his laugh and sneer. It seems impossible that you want him but you do and your pain is the abyss between the strength of your desire and the teasing indifference he pays you.

Perhaps you are losing your touch, perhaps you were getting bored with the same boy in no matter how many guises, but you knew when you saw him, when you first spoke to him in that bar where he was attacking the fruit machine with such energy that you expected the coins to rush out at his feet, you knew then that he was different, that he had no need of your comfort, your money or your company. But you spoke to him and because he did not feel threatened by you, because he knew you could never threaten him, he answered and allowed you to buy him a drink and the evening began there. You took him home and made love with him expertly and after it was over you were surprised, even disappointed, when he said he could not stay. Can I see you again, you asked, not even aware that, although you had heard the words often, it was the first time you had spoken them. He nodded, gave you a time and place, scribbled down his phone number, walked out and you went to bed slightly confused that for the first time in many years there was a space beside you when you had not planned that there would be.

His name is Ian, he claims to be a mechanic, to live in Stoke Newington. You don't quite believe him, listen to his conversation as carefully as a cat watching a mousehole, waiting for a lie to timidly appear so that you can seize it and play with it and toss it up in the air before him. All you hear, however, are stories about his mates, told with laughter that mocks both them and himself, while the inferences that he is a petty thief are yours and yours alone. Yet whether he is honest or a criminal, a worker or a layabout, he is independent, does not need you and will never need you and that is what is so difficult for you to understand, so hard for you to accept.

He arrives on your doorstep, unexpected, walks in without invitation, kisses you, pulls your hand to his crotch and turns away before you can decide whether you are aroused by his presence or angered by his attitude. He makes appointments which he does not keep and makes no apology when next you meet, shrugging off the incident as of no more importance than a beer left half-drunk, a pound lost in gambling. He calls you old, geriatric, past it, insults where the humour is weaker than the doubts which accompany it. It is only in bed, on the few occasions you can persuade him there, that you are equals, that he even submits to you, recognising the proficiency within your narrow and rigid role.

You do not know what he wants from you. It might be your

possessions, your money, but if he were to steal from you he would have done so long ago and never returned; nor is he naive enough to imagine that the closer he — or any other — gets to you, the more likely you are to trust him with your keys and cheque-book, credit cards and safe. It is not your maturity, your wisdom or experience he wants, for he has enough confidence to believe he possesses all he needs, nor your security and reassurance, for his own personality is strong enough to withstand any blows. No, your attraction to him, although he does not think about it, is the effort you make to hide the depths of your desire, to assert control over both yourself and him. It amuses him when you berate him, when you treat him as the child he is not; he almost laughs when you tell him you are busy and he must leave, for he knows how much you want him to stay. In short, he controls you, with a word he can bring joy or desperation to your eyes. It is difficult when you are young to have so much power and not to use it; be grateful that he is not evil, that he does not wish you harm.

From him you do not know what you want or why you want it. Everything about him irritates, angers and fascinates you. You tell yourself you are not attracted and you know that you lie. So you say it is his youth, his firm body and his readiness to rut, but there are thousands of others in London who could fulfil that role. You try to convince yourself you can indeed do something for him, that when he settles down you can finance a garage, a small business, yet your instinct tells you that he would want neither the money you would offer nor the strings that would go with it. So you try to forget him, to refuse to see him, to turn him away, and you find you are unable to do so, you want to know where he is, what he is doing. At odd moments you wonder whether he is indeed in overalls flat on his back under some rusty car or negotiating a van laden with stolen goods through the traffic jams of the West End, whether he is indeed with his mates in some bar and losing money on the machines or with the true lover you sometimes imagine he has, telling him about you and laughing at your expense. Wherever he is, whatever he is doing, you cannot forget him but want, like a child, to be with him.

You ask yourself how and when it will end. It could end when he gets tired of you, which may be soon, today, tomorrow, whenever someone else takes your place as the butt of his interest and amusement. It could, but won't, end the next time you see him, when you tell him as authoritatively as you speak to your staff, as you spoke to his predecessors, not to come back, and place a cheque, not too large, in his hand as on completion of a contract. Most likely, however, is that it will drag on for some time, you will allow yourself to be torn between the habits of a generation and lust for something you dimly recognise you never had. So you will see him again and again and his presence and his body, even his skewed affection, will dance before you as tantalising as a rare butterfly to a collector without a net. While he is there you can, just, accept the pleasure as greater than the pain, but when he goes and you realise that you miss him, that to keep him you would do anything but can do nothing, it is then you really understand what unhappiness is.

A SENSE
OF LOSS

I never spoke to him. And although I knew his name, it was years before I realised who he was. I was in Paris, a student at last, searching for something to read among the *bouquinistes*. A small, thin, unshaven man with a collection that was tired and dog-eared pushed a volume into my hand. "There, sir, you should read this. A marvellous book, the story of our times." It was *The Abject*, an old French edition with a stained and grubby cover. I took it, if only because the price he was asking was the small amount I could afford and showed it to the friend I was with. He nodded absently. "You know him?" I asked. "Of course." I was ashamed of my ignorance and asked what else he had written; there followed several familiar titles. "He died," my friend added, "before the war." It was later that day as I sat down to read that the two facts came together in my mind; I looked at the spine and saw his name, remembered the old man in his chair, the hazy sun, the sea and the sand.

We had been at the hotel for a week when he appeared. Father had insisted on us leaving early that year. It was for my health, he said, but I was old enough to understand that my health was no more than an excuse to send us away. He was proud of his children in his way but he did not quite know how to speak to us, how to treat us. We did not fit into his world of book-lined offices, of stern portraits overlooking industrious young clerks and white-haired old men with ponderous voices. Although he liked me as well as he could, he liked the girls more, perhaps because he had no expectations of them. It was enough that they were pretty and dressed in frills and bows and wore demure expressions when the old ladies of the town stopped to pay compliments. Meanwhile I, the youngest child and the only son, was neither athletic nor studious, humble nor rebellious, displayed no virture he could encourage nor vice he could condemn. We were not disappointments to him but we were an embarrassment, an embarrassment that could be relieved each summer if we were all sent away on the pretext of education or health.

As a small boy I had always loved the train journey, the swaying of the carriages, the clatter of the wheels, the trees and fields rushing past. We children would stand in the corridor with our noses to the window, playing games spotting animals and imagining scenes behind distant hills, or sit in our compartment with enormous serviettes on our knees as Mother handed us bread and pickle and thick slices of ham. Mademoiselle would sit opposite, trying to keep us under control, reminding us of our manners and to keep our clothes clean. For a day and a night, however, our excitement was unrestrained, sleep came reluctantly and routine held no sway.

That year, however, the only games were the riddles and acrostics initiated by Mother and the familiar French memory tests which formed the heart of the education given by Mademoiselle. At our posts in the corridor the girls would not talk to me except to say I should go off on my own. "Find a boy to play with," Maria, the oldest, said several times. "But there are none in this carriage," I told her, "and Mother won't let us go into the others." "Always doing what Mummy says," Olga jeered. "Don't you?" I asked. "Yes, but I'm a girl," she replied with a vehemence that hurt as much as it surprised. For the rest of the long journey I stared at the passing landscape wavering between self-pity and anger, my dislike of being alone, of watching while others talked and laughed, giving way to the hatred I felt for all three sisters. Zosi I could forgive, for she looked at me sympathetically, but Olga I resented most, for she was only a year older and I still thought of her as my closest companion.

At the hotel my mood lifted. We went into dinner the first evening to see people we knew; standing behind Mother as she greeted the Andrzejewskis I smiled at Jaschiu, a boy my age I had met the year before. Of all the children I had liked him best, although at times his constant presence had irritated as much as pleased. There were others I recognised and new families we were sure to get to know, but looking round the dining-room I was aware of slight disappointment, as if I had been expecting someone, an old friend or a new acquaintance, who was not there.

Those first days the weather was dull, the days warm and the evenings cool. After breakfast we would go down to the beach where a parasol and table were set up in front of the cabin and Mother sat with her books and correspondence while Mademoiselle fussed over towels and her handbag and little baskets of sweetmeats and fruit. The girls sat and talked, taking care not to get sand or dirt on the hems of their dresses or over their shoes. It was only later that I realised they did not enjoy themselves as I did; too old to play games, they could only sit and watch or go for walks together along the beach no further than Mother could see. To swim required great preparation, carefully changing in the cabin while Mademoiselle fretted outside, calling to them to check all their buttons and to be sure to pull their bathing caps down, the whole procedure being reversed when they came out of the water. I, meanwhile, was free to go wherever I pleased, to build castles or play tag, to rush into the sea and lie on the sand. There were plenty of children to share games and because I was the tallest and eldest I was never left out, could decide what we all should do. All I had to suffer was Mother's occasional reminders to dry myself thoroughly and not exert myself and even then she spoke gently, encouraged rather than chastised.

At night after dinner we would sit on the terrace or in the lounge. Sometimes I was happy to watch the people around us, to listen to the different languages, the greetings and conversations. I would feel very adult and try to behave with an adult's gravity, speaking slowly and paying great attention to what I said.

My sisters, however, would laugh at my comments and then I would be angry and sit stubbornly silent until Mother made me answer politely or sent me to bed. At other times some of the older children and I would play a quiet form of hide and seek. My favourite refuge was an alcove in a corridor seldom used at night. If Jaschiu was the hunter he knew where to find me and always left me to last. It had taken no time to fall into our old relationship — a few months younger than me, he could never be the older brother I sometimes I wanted, but he was quiet and faithful and I was glad he was there.

I do not know when the old man arrived. He could have been at the hotel for some time, dining in his room, spending each day in town, before the morning that I first noticed him. It was on the beach, I had come out of the water, shivering with cold, with life, wrapped myself in a towel and lay face down in the sand. There, my eyes closed, the sun on my back, my mind was free to wander in that limbo between consciousness and sleep, between indi- viduality and the universal, between awareness and death. The thoughts that came to me in that darkness were not words nor pictures but emotions that were new, that I neither recognised nor understood. More reticent than afraid, I opened my eyes and in the harshness of light saw only one thing, a man in a deck- chair reading a book. He looked older, I now know, than he was; his old-fashioned clothes — the dark trousers and dark shoes, the high collar and sombre hat — the concentration with which he read, the careful manner with which he turned each page, the calm expression with which he occasionally looked up and round, all identified him in my ignorance as one of Father's partners or more venerable clients. At that moment he was unique, the rest of the world a void in which only he floated; unthinkingly I stared until his glance fell on mine. Suddenly aware of my rudeness, I jerked my head away and closed my eyes, returning to the world I had only begun to explore. The day was warm, the swim had tired me, I began to doze; when I woke I had forgotten him and he had gone.

I noticed him later, but no more than I noticed the other hotel guests that I passed in the corridors and lifts and bowed to in the

dining-room. Indeed, I paid him less attention, for being alone
and having no conversation he was duller than most who
surrounded him. One morning I thought he was leaving, for as
I sat late at breakfast I saw him distributing tips and walk out of
the hotel, a travelling-bag in his hand. That night, however, he
was in the dining-room at his usual table by the wall, studying a
German newspaper as he carefully spooned his soup.

He may have glanced at me then but my attention was
elsewhere; I was restless that evening, with no time for others,
irritated by my sisters' gossip and reluctant to join the evening
walk Mother proposed. Sitting back in my chair I looked round
at the tall and wide room, the chandeliers floating above me, the
dark-suited waiters, the tables of guests like lilies floating on a
pond. There were too many people, far too many people; I
wanted to be alone or I wanted to be in darkness or I wanted to
be outside. I did not know what I wanted, only that within me
there was an unsatisfied and unrecognised need, an itch that
tormented just out of reach. I resented having to sit stiffly in stiff
clothes as my sisters laughed their silly laugh, Mother and
Mademoiselle discussed our education and the other guests
around me clinked their cutlery and talked and talked. Oh to be
free, I thought to myself, ignorant of what freedom was, of what
it might be for.

It was the next morning that I realised he was watching me.
We were all on the beach again, except for Maria, who was lying
in her room with a headache. Jaschiu had gone with his family
into town and I was not in the mood to play with the other
children. As Mademoiselle waited for Zosi to change and Mother
and Olga were deep in conversation, I went for a long walk along
the water's edge, kicking each wave as it rushed over my feet.
Whatever I was looking for I did not find and eventually I turned
and walked slowly back towards our cabin, my eyes glancing over
those hotel guests who had come down to sit and talk, crochet
or play games. I saw him before I caught sight of Mother,
recognised the silhouette of his hat and his stiff posture in the
chair, the book on his knees, a page flapping idly against his
hand. I could not see his eyes for the brim cast his face in shadow,

but the closer I approached, the more certain I grew that he was watching me, that every pace I took, every swing of my arms, each movement of my head, even the rise and fall of my breath, was as intense to him as my vision of him had been the other day. I was embarrassed, as if I had been caught wrong-doing, and continued walking only because I was already in movement and did not have to make the effort of decision. At last I had passed him and the heat of his gaze and was safe in Mother's greeting, in Mademoiselle's nervous smile.

Cajoled by Mother, I began to build a sandcastle close to the water's edge. It was no mere mound I wanted, with pretty little turrets and crowned by the flags of Italy and Poland, but an engineering feat, great towers rising above bridges and tunnels and a whole complex of moats. Soon I was surrounded by younger children all wanting to help, most of whom I knew and had played with before. It was my castle, however, and I allowed nothing to be done without my approval, sending those I could not trust to build carefully in search of sticks and card to reinforce the structure. By lunchtime it was complete, less complex than I had wished but nonetheless monumental. As Mother came down to admire it I looked at the deckchair where the old man had sat. It was empty and I was not sure whether I was disappointed or relieved.

We did not leave the hotel very often. On Sundays we went to Mass and stayed in town for a late luncheon or to go for a walk but during the week Mother preferred to sit on the beach, to read and write letters. Besides, she said, the sea air was good for my health, for she was never convinced that the shortness of breath which had attacked me when younger would not return. I thus saw him frequently and each time our paths crossed his eyes met mine. They did not linger, flickered over me and then passed, but it was the strength of the gaze that struck me rather than its duration. Gradually the impression grew that he was judging me, that he knew everything about me, had summed up my history, listed all my faults. He was the tutor displeased with my work, the policeman suspecting me of broken windows, my father disappointed in my lapse of manners. In the hotel I could avoid the confrontation, look down or away each time he approached, but on the beach he could sit for hours, free to cast his glance towards me whenever he wished. I did not know how I had offended, could only reason that it was his revenge for that first day when I had lain on the sand and unthinkingly stared up at him. Now he was punishing me for my rudeness, but doing so excessively, not merely returning one blow for another but hitting me hard again and again.

I wanted him to stop but did not know how to make him do so, thought of telling Mother but did not know what to say. Even as I rehearsed the conversation I knew it sounded ridiculous. One of the hotel guests was watching me? So? Did I not have more reason to fear the manager, whose eye was often on me, annoyed by my more than once running through his hall? Besides, if I could explain, might Mother not take the stranger's view and wish to punish me as well? And if Olga heard, she would only laugh at me, tease me for being frightened by an old man. It was better to say nothing, to hope that he would soon decide I had suffered enough and return his attention to his newspaper, his books and his letters.

He did not, however, and one night when I had a fever after staying too long in the sun I could not drive his face from my mind. I lay in bed, alternately pushing the covers away and pulling them over me, sure he was in the room sitting in the armchair by the door as he sat every day on the beach. I saw his hat, a homburg as neatly creased as his jacket and trousers, his moustache, thick, black and grey, stretching over his lips and onto his cheeks like my father's, and, half-shaded, his eyes, dark, clear, strong, lying below brows that curled into a frown. It was not so much his face I saw as the face of all men, the face of my father when I had done something wrong. Then it was not the punishment I feared but the sense of guilt, my reddening face and perspiration as Father made me wait, gave me time to think over my crime. For the first time, however, I did not know what that crime was, was more than half-convinced that I had done nothing wrong. I had neither lied nor stolen, had not hurt my sisters nor Mother, had studied at school, had not become drunk or smoked any cigarettes. All I had done was stare at someone by mistake; if I could apologise to him I would do so. I could not speak, however, could only watch him in his chair. It seemed that he was closer, that his eyes were stronger and stronger. I could not breathe. I pushed the covers away, tore at the neck of my nightgown. Dimly I was aware that I was ill, should pull the bell-rope and summon Mother, but for once I did not want her, I insisted on seeing this through alone. I saw his eyes, heard Father say "You've done wrong, you've done wrong." I was too hot. I pulled off my nightgown and lay naked on the bed. I was still having difficulty in breathing. Apologise, I told myself, apologise, but when my mouth opened it was to gasp "I did not, I did not." The phrase repeated itself again and again and as it died Father fell silent and the old man returned to his chair.

I opened my eyes to see no one but an empty room, a shaft of moonlight pouring through a gap in the curtain. Aware that I was covered in sweat, I took my nightgown and dried myself down, then stood up to draw the curtain. Curiosity made me open it instead; I looked down onto a deserted beach. The shadows, like a photographic plate, made the scene strangely beautiful. I stared for a while, half expecting movement or change, then turned away, the curtains left open, to look for a fresh nightgown. As I took it out of the drawer, however, I decided I did not want it; for some time it had bothered me like the stiff collar of a clean shirt. But what if Mother were to come in to wake me as she sometimes did? I could lock the door, even though it was expressly forbidden in case I should have another attack. But was I not still weak from gasping on the bed? I had survived without Mother bending over me, without Maria or Zosi rushing in with boiling water and menthol for me to inhale. I had survived and would do so again. Feeling strong, feeling adult, I walked to the door and turned the key, got into bed and pulled the covers over me. As I stretched out and felt the sheets rub against my body it seemed the most delicious thing I could ever do.

Sleep came soon and was untroubled. I woke early, emerging from a dream of deep friendship into a room that was almost unnaturally bright. I remembered the fever and my defiance of the previous night, the old man and his aggressive stare. It was clear now how to resolve the situation — I had only to approach him, speak and apologise if I had offended. Content, my apprehension gone, I stood up and went over to the window. There was no one on the beach apart from a man and a boy setting up parasols and a youth in the distance painting a cabin. I longed to join them, to stroll along the sand and see this different world, to dive into the water and wash away sleep, dirt, my ignorance and childhood, I longed to be a sailor on the fishing boats setting out to sea in the distance, a man amongst men: rugged, strong and tanned. I stood there for a moment and suddenly realised that these wishes were not impossible but might be fulfilled. Not immediately, not this summer, but in a year or two I would be old enough to make my own decisions, to choose my own life. I opened the window and breathed in the sea air, its rumours of salt and travel and foreign lands, of my manhood and my future.

I washed and dressed, walked calmly down to the breakfast-room, prepared to stop, bow, present my apologies, receive his acknowledgement and walk away, my conscience cleared. As I entered, he looked up, kept his eyes on me as I approached. I had to force myself not to look down, not to offer an admission of guilt. I stared back and saw with growing surprise that his expression was not the disapproval or anger I had imagined, was neither hostility nor contempt. It was an emotion I did not recognise, as if he were both amazed and afraid. As I drew closer he looked away and I, disturbed, found myself walking past him, all resolve forgotten, greeting Mother, Zosi and Mademoiselle and sitting down in my usual seat. "Sleep well?" Mademoiselle asked and I nodded, the previous night's attack as far from my mind as if it had never occurred, as if it had been a stranger who had suffered, a character in a book. Mother beckoned the waiter and coffee was poured into my cup, a roll set on my plate, while I sat and tried to understand my feelings, to understand what had happened, what had changed.

From that day on I was continually conscious of his presence, knew that on the beach and at dinner I had only to turn and I would see him, reclining in a deckchair, a book unread on his lap, upright at table, drinking and eating with politeness and care. When my eyes were on him, he would seldom stare directly at me but focus on something nearby. Thus he would seem to be admiring the sandcastle we were building or smiling at one of the younger children, her thumb stuck firmly in her mouth or, at night, he would inspect the flower spray at an adjacent table or wonder which dessert to choose from the tray a waiter offered us. I saw that he did not want to intrude, only wanted me to know that he was there. His expression, meanwhile, softened, lost the intensity I had taken as disfavour, but not the shade of wonder that I still did not quite understand. From Mother I learnt that he was a writer, quite well known, but his conservative dress, his deliberate movements, the quiet voice I sometimes overheard still reminded me more of my father's world. I tried to imagine him at a desk, eyes wild, muttering to himself, scribbling over paper, pausing to think of the next word or phrase, but could not do so. Indeed, I could not imagine him anywhere other than here, at any other activity than rest, his attention anywhere except on me.

I did not know why he watched me but I accepted that in doing so he wished me well and not harm. There was in his gaze a mystery and I could not see where it rested, in him or in me or somewhere between the two. It was enough to know that it existed, that I had a secret which no one suspected, which, I told myself, was far greater than the secrets of children in any book I had read, far greater than the quiet discussions in the library between Mother and Father after the four of us had gone to bed. I had grown old enough to learn that even to admit the existence of something concealed is to reveal it, so I said nothing, for there was no one I wanted to share this mystery with. Even the old man I seemed to ignore but it was not chance that led me to play near him when we could have played anywhere, to run past him on my way to or from the water, to dawdle when we met in corridors. Sometimes I sensed him before he appeared, looked up to see him entering the room, turned to discover him walking behind

me. Once, when Mother had taken us into town and I had not
seen him for a day, he was waiting as we returned to the hotel.
I smiled as I might have greeted an old friend. It was a mistake;
he frowned as if I had gone too far, turned aside and walked
away.

Yet much of the time I forgot him, thought only of the beach,
what I had done there one day and would do the next. Mother
seemed to think I would be happy there and for much of the time
I was; I loved the warmth, to run along the water's edge or rush
in, to mould the sand into taller and more precarious structures,
to lie on the beach and eat strawberries and peaches, bananas
and oranges. At times too, it was fun to play with the other
children, to tease the younger ones then make them laugh, but
often I wanted to be alone and resented Mother's and Mademoiselle's prompting to join the others, to start a new game. The
only companion I was happy to be with most of the time was
Jaschiu, although even he at times irritated with his eagerness to
please. When I was bored or felt moments of anger or resentment with Mother he and I would walk along the beach and talk
about leaving the hotel together, making our way in the world as
two adventurers. He would be the fighter and I would be the
planner; we would travel from country to country living as
gypsies, making our fortune. At other times we would sit and talk
more realistically — his quarrelling parents, his future in the
army and the rank he might reach, my sisters and the years
before us. Girls had begun to intrigue him whereas they still
made me uncertain; he eagerly repeated tales of his older
brother's exploits as I listened, both curious and mistrustful.

Time passed, day after day punctuated by meals and changes
of clothes, by trips into Venice and letters from Father. Perhaps
it is only memory that tells me the old man was getting tired, that
the book on his lap as he sat in his deckchair remained un-
opened, that the food set before him each evening in the dining-
room was only listlessly eaten. A greyness seemed to hang over
him as it hung over Venice, offering us warm, sultry days in
which the sun shone but never appeared. Perhaps I am anticipat-
ing, misinterpreting what I saw later. At that time I had not

grown tired of his attention, our occasional exchange of glances, but I sometimes acknowledged him in the same spirit that I received others' compliments, with more indifference than gratitude. "What a handsome boy!" Mother's friends would say and I would smile and try not to fidget, pretend I was not eager to get away. Yet if after a day or two it seemed that I had ignored him, I would be disturbed, unable to rest until he came into view again and I could half-smile or pass by his seat in an obvious detour.

One Sunday we went to Mass as usual and I knew he had followed us. The service was long, as befitted a cathedral; towards the end as the others bowed their head in prayer I only half leant forward, left my eyes open. It was a moment of freedom, defiance, before Olga whispered a reproach at me in a voice whose sharpness would carry to Mother. I turned, looked over the row upon row of curved and motionless backs, and saw him sitting bolt upright, his head bare, his face upon me. There was a quite different expression in his eyes, a look of pain and supplication, of desire and need similar to the hunger I had seen in beggars and yet quite different. Troubled, I turned back and bent my head, less from piety than to give me time to think. I did not know the meaning of what I had seen and it frightened me in ways that I did not understand. I felt I was being asked for something I could not give, something much greater than I possessed; if I had been older or more precocious I might have called it my soul. Yet with that fear there came a thrill, that what I had seen was denied to the rest of the world, that his entreaty was at the same time a gift so precious that it could not be refused.

After Mass Mother told us she was tired and was going back to the hotel. I hoped she would take Mademoiselle and allow me to be my sisters' chaperon, but instead she was instructed to take us on a walk through the city. I loitered behind, tired of my sisters' chatter and Mademoiselle's repeated warnings of loose stones, of rusty handrails and dirt on the streets. I knew that I would not be alone, that whatever drew the old man to me had become much stronger, that we met by design and no longer by chance. Reluctantly, I kept Mademoiselle and my sisters in sight as we crossed steep bridges and turned blind corners, stopped to look at shop windows and stall-holders' wares, peered inside churches and read the inscriptions on statues and busts. Each time the others' attention was elsewhere I looked round and saw him. He seldom stared at me directly but engaged in sightseeing as assiduously as we, only occasionally allowing himself to look in my direction. Then, for a timeless moment, we would stare at each other, no expression on our faces, waiting for I know not what, until, conscious of convention and reality, one or other of us would jerk our gaze away.

That night I lay awake for hours trying to understand what I had seen. In the dimness of my youth I knew that he needed me, but I lacked the imagination to tell me what that need was, to tell me what in such a situation I could and should do. Nor did it occur to me that such a position gave me privilege, that power, if only the power to turn him away, lay in my hands. When at last I fell asleep I dreamt of him, the first of many intense visions that neither pleased nor disturbed, scenes in which he approached me, standing so close that our bodies almost touched. I waited then for something to happen but nothing did, wanted to speak to him but found my voice gone. I listened, sure he was trying to tell me something; as curious as I was to hear it I was also afraid. He said not a word. These dreams came and went as did others at that time, dreams that I now know all boys have, dreams which filled me with excitement and guilt. Sleep had become inviting, no longer an interruption to the day; at the end of each evening I left the others to come upstairs, open the curtains, lock the door, throw off my clothes and enter my private world, a world which at times offered so much more than the one in which I lived.

I had heard but paid little attention to rumours of sickness in the city. It was only after I wondered aloud one morning whether the Grünwalds, an Austrian family with whom we had some connection, would be coming that Maria told me, beyond Mother's hearing, of the cholera that was keeping many away. It did not occur to me then to wonder why we did not leave, nor that Mother, usually so concerned about our health, seemed happy to stay. When, much older, I asked her about it, she said Father had been expected to join us and she had not wanted the upheaval of leaving one hotel and city to settle down in another. It was also not good, she added, for Poles to be seen running away. So we stayed and each day the dining-room was emptier, the tennis-court seldom played and fewer cabins open on the beach. Vendors no longer wandered past, confident of custom, but stopped to put down their baskets and pester us with their wares; gondoliers called out to us, reducing their prices as we walked by; the old cabin attendant muttered to his grandson that times were bad and, although he had more time, served us with less and less grace. I noticed the changes but was not disappointed, the fewer people that were around me the more time I had for myself. Nor was I afraid, for I saw the disease as the creature of darkness and dirt, lurking in slums and corners where I would never go.

I might be healthy, but the old man had begun to look ill. His face was drawn, his colour sallow, yet his dress had begun to change. A new suit made an appearance, lighter in colour and more modern in cut, his stiff hat was replaced by one of felt; rings sat on his fingers, a flower in his lapel and a coloured handkerchief in his breast pocket. With each addition he glanced longer in my direction; our eyes met and locked like metal to a magnet until it became an effort to tear myself away. His look still begged but was underlain by a complex of feelings that I did not understand. Too young then to read his face, I am too old now to remember it well. Perhaps there was gratitude for my recognition, perhaps defiance or anger, apology or despair. Whatever his emotion, I never resented it, for under his eyes I shivered, a sensation as keen and as delicate as when I was naked and alone. Furthermore, I had begun to need his presence as an addict needs his opium, checking frequently that he was there, allowing my eyes to rest on him as if by doing so I could read not only his mind but my own, could understand this situation we found ourselves in. I learnt nothing, however, for his face was like a Chinese character whose lines continually intrigue but whose message only initiates can understand, yet I never ceased to search.

Whatever changes he made, I was not prepared for the one to come. Going into dinner one evening, the last of our party, I looked as usual at his table and was shocked to see a stranger, a younger man with dark and unnaturally bright hair, red complexion and puffy cheeks, eyes sunk under thick black brows. A man both untrustworthy and effeminate, I told myself. Yet even as that opinion was forming I saw who he was. There was no time to wonder at his motives, for as Mother passed he looked up and saw me. Even in my youth I could understand the expression that struggled through the make-up. "I have done this for you," it said. "Do you like it? Please, please tell me you do." Stunned, my mouth dry and my heart pounding, I passed him; his face, released from the gravity of my presence, fell. I sat down, unable to look in his direction, wondering if the others noticed my shaking and guessed the reason why.

The meal that followed was the longest and most painful I can remember. I wanted to run away from everyone, run away from these people and these lights and run away and lock myself into my room. There I would cry, shout, beat my bed, laugh, scream, do whatever act was necessary to expel this violent emotion surging up within me stronger than any I had ever known. Only then, when I lay drained, exhausted, would I be able to think about what had happened, to explain my sense of betrayal, begin to understand what it meant. But I could not move. I could only sit and be polite to Mother, listen to my sisters and keep my eyes adverted while he sat, like a snake that had crawled back into his shedded skin, little more than twenty feet away. Trapped, held down, at that moment I hated everyone in my family, Mother for her insistence on decorum and manners, Mademoiselle for her nerves and puffy fat face, my sisters for their giggling and gossip and teasing. It was because of them that I was sitting there suffering, that I was not free to do what I wanted. They were strangers who knew nothing about me, nothing about life and I hated their existence and my dependence on them.

That night in my room I dreamt of him. He came to me on the

beach, the young man with the old man's eyes, reached out an
arm to rest it on my shoulder, brought his face to mine to
whisper in my ear. I wanted him close to me and yet I was afraid,
wanted something from him without knowing what. Impercep-
tibly he changed, became a being that was both young and old,
male and female. Then I wanted to embrace him, to hold him
close to me; I reached out to put my arms around him. My whole
body touched his, we kissed, fervently, but in that kiss he faded
and I woke to find myself clasping the bolster and the covers
twisted and half off the bed.

The next morning when I went into breakfast he was there.
The hair was still thick and black but the bright colour had faded
from his face. He looked up, his expression more hopeful, less
pleading than the night before. My reaction was mixed; a return
of the curiosity of earlier days and a pity and contempt. I did not
understand where the latter emotions came from, nor how they
could coexist. Perhaps they reflected in my face, for I found I
could not smile when I passed him, could only look away, think
about greeting Mother, sitting down, drinking coffee and who
would be on the beach that day.

The rest of the week passed. Despite my new ambivalence
towards him I found that I was restless in his absence, could only
relax if he was near. I was short-tempered on the beach, quiet at
dinner, if he was not there. Olga's sarcasm was aroused but if the
others noticed my moodiness they ignored it, ascribed it no
doubt to my youth and sex. On Sunday we went to Mass and for
a long walk afterwards. I had hoped he would not follow but was
glad when he did, then concerned when I saw how slowly he
walked, as if he were tired or ill. Eventually he lost us, for Mother
was quicker than Mademoiselle and insisted on leading us down
narrow streets where we had never been. It was our last chance
to see much of the city, she explained, for we were to leave on
Thursday; Father was staying in Warsaw, had heard of the
cholera and told us to come home. Despite myself I welcomed
the news, for I had become bored with Venice, had no more
enthusiasm for the beach or the sea. I would miss Jaschiu,
perhaps, and the greater freedom I had here. As for the old man,

I had mixed feelings. Leaving him would be at once a great loss and a burden lifted, but the burden at that moment was far greater than the reward.

It was Mother's words and the knowledge of our departure that gave me the freedom to see him differently, as a casual acquaintance and not a secret conspirator. Dispassion lent the edge of cruelty, allowed me to dismiss him as a nobody, a man without friends, without family or reputation. His face was lined, the skin thick, his jaw sagged. His older clothes were out of fashion, the new ones he had bought did not fit well. He ate like a woman, carefully and delicately; he walked like an old man, hesitant where I strode. He read and wrote nothing, drank little and smoked only small cigars; my father was superior to him in every way. Yet each time I looked at him part of me was still drawn, saw him as someone I wished to talk to and know, someone who in a way far beyond me was more significant than all the bustling and chattering guests around him. Perhaps the failure did not lie in him but me, and whenever I thought so I looked towards him and tried to apologise.

On Wednesday evening Mademoiselle came in and helped me to pack, leaving out a travelling-bag with my bathing costume and a change of clothes. After breakfast the next morning Olga, Mother and I went down to the beach. He came down later and sat in his usual chair, looking much older and tired. There were few people on the sands. Jaschiu and two or three others were there; we started splashing water at each other; inadvertently I threw some sand which hit him in the face. I laughed, he grew angry and would not accept my apology. He leapt on me and I realised how much stronger, more masculine, he was. I could not fend off his hands, his head, his knees, but found myself falling to the ground. He pushed me over, sat on my back and pulled an arm up so hard I thought it would break. I shouted at him, begged for mercy through tears, but he pushed my face into the sand so that I could not breathe. Frightened, in pain, I bucked to shake him off, but he was too heavy and I could only lie and think I was going to die. At last he let go and I sat up, exhausted, in pain, my mouth full of grit; the anger and hurt I felt almost physical. I stood up and walked away, ignoring him when he ran after me, stood at the water's edge wondering what to do, where to go. I did not want to stay here, did not want to go home, did not want to do anything.

I walked into the water and as I did so noticed that it had receded, leaving ahead of me an island of sand. I turned and pointed it out to the others but they did not respond. I walked forward, swam a few strokes and climbed up onto the sandbar; from here I had a clearer view of the beach and hotel. It was my little kingdom and I wanted to stay for ever; my family could go and leave me alone. I walked the length of my small domain and as I turned back saw a cluster of people around the old man's chair. Afraid, I ran into the water, cursed its slowing me, tried to swim, stood up again and at last made it to the beach. As I ran up I saw Mother's figure, heard her taking command. I stopped running, knowing what had happened and not knowing how I felt. Olga turned and saw me coming. "It's Mr Aschenbach," she whispered. "I think he's dead."

I peered over shoulders and caught a glimpse of a pale drawn face slumped to the side, eyes half-closed, saliva dribbling from the corner of the mouth. I thought it cruel and vulgar that so many people should stand and stare and turned away to walk back to the sea. I should be sad, I thought, in tears, but my eyes remained dry; I knew I had lost something but did not know what and that, somehow, made the pain easier to bear.

Robert Farrar
STATE OF INDEPENDENCE

"The story of how I lost that which can never be regained — my innocence — has amused many a dinner party of bright young same-sexers in the Hammersmith and Shepherds Bush neck of the woods."

Fresh from the reclusion of the Home Counties, the impressionable Lenny relates his own dizzying introduction to London's energetic gay scene, cynically observing the sexual exploits of others while secretly pining away for an unrequited love. Submerged in the hedonistic nightlife and exhausting antics of his flatmates, Lenny seeks a place for himself that escapes both the oppression of his parents' religion and the frenzy of the disco jungle.

"At last a gay coming-of-age narrative for adults! Robert Farrar's debut novel takes a pleasingly irreverent, rancid view of gay London. ... *State of Independence* will bring a blush to the cheek of anyone who was ever young, embarrassed or evangelically Christian."

— Patrick Gale

ISBN 0 85449 194 5
UK £6.95   US $12.95   AUS $19.95

Steven Corbin
FRAGMENTS THAT REMAIN

"It's one thing to be called a nigger by a stranger. Quite another when you're sleeping with him."

Skylar Whyte's success doesn't come easy, especially for a black American — a movie actor with a career and a lover. Yet despite all his triumphs he is inwardly tormented, not just by the racism he still encounters in daily life, but by memories of a bullying father himself destroyed by white society.

Steven Corbin shows a strength and conviction in depicting both the horrors and the joys of gay life for black Americans today. He is the author of *No Easy Place to Be*, and his short fiction has appeared in GMP's *More Like Minds*.

ISBN 0 85449 186 4
UK £8.95   AUS $24.95

GMP books can be ordered from any bookshop in the UK, and from specialised bookshops overseas. If you prefer to order by mail, please send full retail price plus £2.00 for postage and packing to:

GMP Publishers Ltd (GB),
P O Box 247, London N17 9QR.

For payment by Access/Eurocard/Mastercard/American Express/Visa, please give number and signature.
A comprehensive mail-order catalogue is also available.

In North America order from Alyson Publications Inc.,
40 Plympton St, Boston, MA 02118, USA.
(American Express not accepted)

In Australia order from Bulldog Books,
P O Box 155, Broadway, NSW 2007, Australia.

Name and Address in block letters please:

Name
_____

Address
_____

_____

_____